PLANE LOVE

A Sweet Romance

Billionaire's Bet

Book 4

A.B. Proebstel

ISBN-13: 978-1-946292-09-4

ISBN-10: 1-946292-09-5

Printed in the United States of America

First Printing, 2020

Second Printing, 2023

Website: https://geni.us/LOA-Home
BookBub: https://geni.us/BBFollow
Goodreads: www.goodreads.com/aproebstel
Facebook: https://geni.us/FB-LOA
X: https://geni.us/Amy-T
Instagram: www.instagram.com/amyproebstel

Books in the Billionaire's Bet Series

DEDICATION

First of all, this book is dedicated to my friends and family. Your support in helping me carve out time to write and your encouragement to keep me going even when life got in the way, has been utterly amazing. I've been so inspired by your thoughtfulness and I hope it shows in my writing.

Secondly, to the readers of this series, I greatly appreciate all of your kind words, amazing reviews, and support along the way. None of this would be possible without your enthusiasm for the characters and their stories.

CHAPTER 1

RICHARD

The scorching Texas sun beat down on Richard as he sat at the outdoor table, eagerly awaiting the arrival of his hickory slow-smoked beef short ribs drenched in mouthwatering sweet and spicy sauce.

The sizzling aroma teased his senses, momentarily distracting him from the whirlwind of emotions stirring inside.

Lillith's recent flirtations with the gym trainer had taken him on an unexpected journey down memory lane. He should be relieved she was directing her attention elsewhere.

Yet it still stung.

His phone chimed with an unread message, as if adding insult to injury, reminding him of the day he stumbled upon Lillith's deceitful texts to her friends.

He thanked his lucky stars for that accidental glimpse into her true intentions. It had been a wake-up call, revealing her intentions to marry him solely for his wealth, he might have been stuck with the gold-digger for life, or worse, for decades of alimony payments. The warning signs had been there all along, but he had brushed them aside under his father's enthusiastic approval of Lillith and her influential family.

Still, he hadn't quite let go of the crushing dagger-to-the-heart feeling, which dug a little deeper when he unexpectedly saw her in the gym. As if fate were toying with him, he had just finished his bench press, narrowly avoiding a disastrous accident over his chest.

Escaping unnoticed, he fled to the locker room, grabbed his gym bag, and slipped out of a side exit, wanting to avoid any confrontation with Lillith. He couldn't help but imagine the dramatic scene she would have caused had she spotted him.

Driving away from the gym, Richard couldn't help but wonder if Lillith had spotted his distinctive black Rolls Royce Phantom in the parking lot. The rarity of such a car in the area made it hard to miss. He contemplated his friend Markson's offer to buy it, thinking that maybe it was time for a change. Markson would probably jump at the chance if he mentioned it.

A new gym was definitely in order; he couldn't risk running into Lillith again. Her relentless calls had only ceased four months ago, probably because she found a new target. Good riddance, he thought, relieved to be free of her clutches.

But the day wasn't over yet, and his phone continued to pester him with notifications, the lock screen filled with unread messages until he flipped the phone over on the table.

Could this day get any worse?

As the server approached with his platter of ribs, he couldn't help but forget his troubles for a moment. The tantalizing aroma made his mouth water, and he was eager to dig in.

"Can I get you anything else?" she asked, scanning the area to see if anyone needed her.

"Not at all, everything's perfect. Thanks," he assured the flustered server, who blushed.

Richard's attention was entirely on the scrumptious ribs before him. He didn't care that she'd forgotten his coleslaw or that she brought him a sweet tea rather than the cola he'd ordered. Now that his favorite dish sat in front of him, he didn't want another interruption until he licked the bones clean. The tantalizing meat coated in the savory sauce called to him, and he couldn't wait to savor every bite.

The waitress heaved a sigh of relief as she hurried over to a nearby table where three mischievous toddlers had just knocked over a pitcher of water. Their gleeful laughter turned into bawling howls as their parents scolded them, and the commotion quickly disrupted the peaceful ambiance of the outdoor dining area.

The mom jumped up, knocking her chair backward as the water soaked through her entire front. She scolded the waitress for being too slow in getting her a dry towel. The relative peacefulness of the outdoor dining fled in an instant of chaos.

Richard couldn't help but chuckle inwardly at the scene. "Well, at least it's a warm afternoon," he thought, imagining that a cool dousing wouldn't be all that bad at the moment.

As he tried to refocus on his own table, his phone continued to ping incessantly with messages from his executive assistant, Brandy. Richard couldn't help but be annoyed at the frivolous interruptions. "Can't I have a lunch hour all to myself?" he grumbled, swiping the screen to see what urgent matter required twenty-three text messages in a mere ten minutes.

"You have got to be kidding me," Richard muttered in disbelief. One message after another extolled the virtues of Brandy's latest fling. Only this time, the guy managed to find the one thing Brandy found irresistible. Sailing. Unbelievably, she accepted his invitation to sail around the world and already left. "I guess today can get worse."

Richard ran his fingers through his slightly disheveled hair, wincing at the sweaty strands. Having left the gym in haste, he hadn't bothered to shower or change his clothes. In his current state, nobody would give him a second glance, unlike when he usually donned his impeccable custom-tailored Alexander Amosu Vanquish suits.

Slamming his phone down onto the table, Richard was determined to push all thoughts of Brandy, Lillith, and his father's incessant advice out of his mind. Right now, he needed to focus on filling his empty stomach. The relief of Brandy leaving, despite the inconvenience, rushed through him. At least he wouldn't have to deal with her drama and find a way to fire her without legal repercussions.

With a sigh, he realized he'd have to ask one of his sales team members to step in for Brandy until he found a replacement.

He preferred a lean staff, but this sudden departure left him in a bind. As much as his father criticized his small team, Richard remained steadfast in his decision. Maxwell Kingston might have a successful CPA firm, but he didn't understand the complexities of running an international luxury airplane manufacturing company like Kingston Air.

His father's constant comparisons to his brother's success in the family business had become tiresome. Richard was determined to prove himself, to show that he could make his own mark in the world. He had no desire to be stuck behind a desk pushing papers eighty hours a week for overly-entitled customers; he wanted to soar, quite literally. Building the world's most exclusive jets was his passion, and he relished the challenge.

Richard didn't need his father's advice on how to run his company or who he should marry. He was determined to make it on his own terms, even if it meant facing constant comparisons and criticism. He'd prove to his family, especially his father and brother, that he could achieve greatness in his own way. And the best part? He'd wake up every day excited to go to work, knowing he was living his dream.

Lifting the first rib to his mouth, Richard's taste buds erupted in delight as he savored the smoky, succulent flavor. All thoughts of discord and comparison fled from his thoughts as he single-mindedly consumed his lunch. The generous amount of sauce used by the pitmaster made him thank his lucky stars that he was still dressed in his gym clothes, sparing him the hassle of expensive dry-cleaning.

Yet, as he relished the meal, his mind couldn't help but wander back to the laundry that Brandy was supposed to have taken care of. He bet she hadn't even left the pick-up slip for him to find. The thought of dealing with the mundane details that Brandy had usually handled grated on his nerves.

Just then, a commotion down the block caught his attention, providing a welcome distraction. His dark thoughts vanished as he watched a pack of dogs excitedly pulling a young lady behind them. He couldn't help but be amused by the scene, and he sat back to enjoy the show, wiping the sticky sauce from his fingers with the oversized napkin.

Her blonde ponytail swaycd back and forth as she turned to speak with the fluffy little dog falling behind the rest of the larger ones leading the charge down the sidewalk. It was hard to believe such a small-framed woman could maintain control, limited as it was, yet the dogs seemed content with the pace she set.

Her face lit up with joy as she interacted with the dogs, and it was evident she loved her job. Richard couldn't help but be captivated by her. The woman wore a uniform with the name of a dog-walking service emblazoned in bold pink letters outlined in black.

As he continued to watch her, thoroughly entertained, he failed to notice the rottweiler that had approached him. The large dog's paws landed on his chest, and before he knew it, its massive tongue was giving him an unexpected slobbery greeting. Richard's surprise was evident, and the unexpected encounter left him momentarily stunned.

"Down! Reba! No!" the woman called out, her eyebrows lowering, and her bottom lip instantly got caught up between her teeth as she pulled the dog away from him. "I'm so sorry! I can pay for dry cleaning. Please, sir. I'm so sorry. I don't know what got into Reba. She's normally so shy and reserved."

As Richard wiped the dog slobber and streaks of barbecue sauce off his cheek, he couldn't help but chuckle at the woman's apologetic expression. "No need to worry. Reba seems to have a taste for the rib sauce here," he quipped with a grin, holding up the napkin as evidence of the canine's culinary preferences. "No harm done."

The dogs continued to surround them, and Reba, undeterred by the scolding, managed to snatch a leftover bone from Richard's plate.

"Reba! No!" Anne-Marie's attempts to retrieve it were thwarted by the leashes and the other dogs' playful antics. "Oh, my gosh. I'm so going to get fired for this! I'm so sorry, sir."

"I promise it's fine," Richard reassured her, amused by the chaos unfolding before him. "I was finished anyway, and that bone only had a little sauce left on it. It won't hurt her to gnaw on it."

Standing up, he introduced himself, "I'm Rich, by the way," though he belatedly realized his fingers were still sticky with sauce.

Without any hesitation, she shook his hand firmly, her lips pulling back politely while her eyes betrayed her confusion and concern. "I'm Anne-Marie." She quickly scolded Reba again, who seemed unperturbed and continued to gnaw on the bone. "I can't believe you, Reba. That was terrible manners."

The dog moved until she was in the shadow of the table, the bone nestled between her front paws. She didn't even look up from her contented bone gnawing with the sides of her back teeth.

As Richard pondered his chance encounter with Anne-Marie, a light bulb of opportunity flickered in his mind. "Do you believe in fate?" he asked suddenly, hoping to convey his genuine interest.

"What? You're not hitting on me right now, are you?"

"No!" He held up his hands as if to ward her off and realized how rude that gesture seemed. The expression transforming her face confirmed he had offended her. "Sorry, I'd like to, but that's not what I meant at all. Ugh. This isn't coming out right. Let me start over." He closed his eyes and took a deep breath.

With composure regained, he continued, "You mentioned needing this job, and I just happen to know of a really good place to work that's hiring. Would you be interested?"

Anne-Marie's eyes narrowed, and her head cocked to the side. "You're not one of those creepy photographers, are you?"

Richard couldn't help but laugh. Where did she come up with this stuff? "No. Not at all. Have you ever heard of Kingston Air?"

"No. I'm not from around here. I just moved to town."

"Oh, no bother. Here," Richard said with enthusiasm, reaching into his gym bag to retrieve a business card. He handed it to her, adding, "The executive assistant just quit today, and we're in desperate need of a replacement. If you're interested, give this number a call, and we can arrange an interview."

Though her fingers hovered close to the card, she hesitated, expressing doubt about her qualifications. "I don't have any office experience. I doubt I'd qualify."

With a determined look, Richard pressed the business card into Anne-Marie's hand, urging her to seize the opportunity. "Trust me; the last girl wasn't qualified either, but she managed just fine. You'll do great," he reassured her, a glint of excitement in his eyes.

He then realized he was running late and had to get back to work. He grabbed his bag and slung it over his shoulder. "I don't mean to be rude, but I've got to run," he explained apologetically. "Don't wait too long to call. This could be your chance for something amazing."

As he hurried away, he almost stumbled over a playful dog darting in front of him. Collecting himself, he made his way to where his Phantom was parked. Richard was glad that Anne-Marie didn't witness him getting into his fancy car; he didn't want to overwhelm her.

Nonetheless, he couldn't shake off the feeling that he needed to do more to encourage her. Maybe revealing that he owned Kingston Air would help break down any barriers. He decided that if he didn't hear from her by the end of the next business day, he'd make a discreet inquiry at the dog-walking shop to find a way to reach her again.

CHAPTER 2

ANNE-MARIE

The card felt like a lead weight in her palm. Conflicting emotions raced through Anne-Marie's mind. Was that guy for real, or was he some sort of creeper?

She flipped over the business card and realized it was made from some lightweight aluminum rather than thick cardstock.

Kingston Air, the Finest Aircraft Worldwide.

A raise would undoubtedly come in handy right now. The landlord raised her rent for the second month in a row. If she didn't know better, she'd say the guy was almost begging her to move out. Nothing had gone according to plan since moving here from Oregon.

There was no way she was going to admit that her mother was right. Leaving all of her friends and family behind to chase after a cowboy had been a colossally bad idea. No sooner had she landed in Houston did she discover Daniel had no intention of honoring his word to help her or be with her. He hadn't even come to the airport to pick her up.

Standing on the curb with her luggage, she'd received a text message saying he didn't have time to get her. Not realizing what she was getting herself into, she'd hailed a cab and went to the address he'd put on the one and only card he'd sent her. It had been a long-shot, but it proved to be the correct place. Eager to surprise Daniel, she rushed up the two flights of stairs to get to his apartment.

She didn't even have to knock to let herself in; the door stood wide open. Just as she opened her mouth to announce her presence, she spotted Daniel lying on the couch with another woman. They were so busy kissing, neither one of them ever knew she had arrived.

Beyond mortified, Anne-Marie refused to dignify her presence to the scoundrel as she retraced her steps back to the parking lot. Her only lucky break was that the cab driver hadn't left. Leaning against the side of the cab, he exhaled smoke and nodded in her direction.

"Can you take me to a cheap motel?" she asked, stopping in front of him.

"Didn't work out, huh?" He lifted his chin toward the apartment.

"Not at all."

"Are you heading back to the airport then?"

"No. I can't go back right now. I just need someplace cheap to stay until I can get a job."

Dropping his cigarette and grinding it into the pavement with his heel, he grabbed her bag. "Hop in, and we'll get going."

Such was her introduction to Houston, and not much else had been any easier. Only the warm weather and her pride kept her from returning to Oregon. This was supposed to be her grand adventure, the once-in-a-lifetime opportunity to be with an awesome guy. He turned out to be a jerk, but that didn't mean she'd waste the trip. Never having been anywhere outside of Oregon, she wanted to explore—see the sights, enjoy the culture.

Unfortunately, reality caught up to her all too soon. She worked for two days as a waitress before they asked her not to come back. Not that she blamed them. The two customers who had worn their meals were probably relieved not to have to deal with her again.

When she discovered Beatrice's Dog Walkers on her way out of the diner, she took a chance and asked if they were hiring. God seemed to smile on her that day; they just had someone quit. She got the job on the spot, along with a uniform and sixteen unruly dogs nobody else wanted to walk.

She didn't mind in the least. As soon as they were out of sight of the shop windows, she dropped down to her knees with the dogs swarming around her. Several of them nipped at her hair, but she knew how to handle them. Within a few minutes, they'd come to an agreement, and she finished her shift. Beatrice had been pleasantly surprised when they all returned happy and worn out.

Yet all of this walking only pointed out how ill-equipped her shoes were. She'd have to spend some of her precious money to invest in better footwear. Already, she felt several blisters under the ball of her left foot after traversing nearly four miles on the hot sidewalks.

The lonely days passed uneventfully, especially after she told Daniel to lose her number. Until today. Until Rich handed her this unusual business card. Could this be another sign from God that she should make another change in her life? Maybe she'd ask Beatrice about it when she got back to the shop.

Besides, she'd have to fess up about Reba's antics. She felt honor-bound to say something before Rich could call in and complain. That would be the worst.

Beatrice held out her hand for the business card after Anne-Marie told her everything. She weighed the card in her palm and whistled appreciatively. "Girl, if you can get a job there, it's like winning the lottery. You need to call them right now." She picked up the phone and held it toward Anne-Marie.

Laughing nervously, Anne-Marie held out her hands as if to ward off something terrible. "You can't be serious. I wouldn't just up and leave you like that. No way. Besides, I told Rich that I don't have the right experience. It would be a waste of everyone's time."

"Nonsense. Let them decide. Besides, after your interview, you can tell me all about what it looks like in there. I've always wanted to see it, but it's closed to the general public. I've heard it's pretty darn fancy, though. Especially since they cater to all of the uppity-ups."

"Wow, when you put it like that, then I'd have to give it a hard no. You've seen what I wear to work. I don't have anything fancy or nice to wear. I certainly can't afford to go shopping. I can barely afford to pay the stupid rent."

Beatrice dropped the card on the desk between them, where it rang out with a metallic clang. She leaned back in her chair. Crossing her arms, she scowled. "I'd say you're too scared to try. What if you found the perfect man there? What about this Rich guy you said Reba attacked? Maybe he's into you after all."

Anne-Marie felt her cheeks get warm at the very notion of Rich wanting anything to do with her. "Reba didn't attack him, don't even put that out there. Besides, I think that guy was a mechanic or something. He certainly wasn't interested in me; he made that abundantly clear."

"Do you have something against mechanics?"

"After Daniel? Maybe. He turned out to be pretty awful."

"Listen, I can't force you to call, but I can tell you that you'd always wonder what could have happened if you would have called. Besides, if they're as desperate as you said they were to get an executive assistant, you could probably ask for a sign-on bonus. Then we could go shopping together, and you can tell me all about what it's like in there."

"You're not going to let this go. Are you?"

"Not on your life. Heck, I'm half-tempted to call the number myself and go in your place if you're determined to squander this opportunity." Beatrice leaned forward to reach for the card.

Without thinking, Anne-Marie snatched it up. "I'm going to think about it. Maybe I'll call tomorrow."

"Tomorrow might be too late. Just call." Beatrice dropped the cordless phone onto the desk and stood. "I'll give you some privacy. I see Mrs. Pringle just pulled up to get Georgie."

"Really subtle, Beatrice," Anne-Marie quipped. Her fingers gripped the edges of the card until it left an imprint in her flesh. Biting her bottom lip, she hesitated to pick up the phone. Could Beatrice be right? If she waited until tomorrow, would it be too late?

Her fingers trembled as she held the phone. It took two tries before she managed to dial the number correctly. On the third ring, she started to pull the phone away from her ear. This was a bad idea. The worst idea ever. Fate was giving her the chance to hang up before she made a bigger fool of herself.

"Anne-Marie? Is that you?" a man's voice asked through the receiver.

Beyond surprised to be called by name, Anne-Marie very nearly dropped the phone. "How did you know it was me?" Dumb! Why had she asked that?

"The caller ID said Beatrice's Dog Walkers. Are you calling to get an interview?"

"How are you doing? I was hoping you didn't have any issues with Reba's incident today." What in the world was she babbling on about? Why didn't she just say yes? Thank goodness they weren't on a video call, or he'd see her flaming pink cheeks.

"As I said earlier, it was nothing. About the interview?"

"Yes, about the interview. When would you like me to come in?"

"How about now? I can send a car to pick you up, or I can pay for you to grab a driver. Are you free right now?"

"Wow, okay. Slow down a little. Things can't be that desperate over there."

"You have no idea. The phones keep ringing off the hook, and the sales guy has no idea what to do with half of the calls. It's a mess. Do you want me to send a car?"

"No, thank you." Glancing at her watch, she calculated how long it would take her to get home, change into something more appropriate, and then call a cab. "I need to swing by my place to change—"

"Don't bother; what you were wearing was fine. I promise."

"My neon pink shirt? You've got to be kidding me right now. Rich, maybe this is a bad idea. I don't think you really want me fumbling around as an executive assistant or even a janitor. I'm sorry to waste your time." Before she could reconsider, she pressed the button to end the call. Breathing in raggedly, she dropped the receiver on Beatrice's desk. Just as she stood to leave, Beatrice entered the office.

"Did you call?"

Anne-Marie nodded, biting her bottom lip to keep it from quivering. Nothing could stop the tear from dropping down her cheek.

"Hey! What's wrong? Did he say something rude to you? Give me that card; I'm going to give him a piece of my mind."

Her ponytail whipped from side to side as she continued to clutch the metal. "No, I told him I changed my mind."

"Well, call him again and change your mind back. Simple." Beatrice picked up the phone and hit redial. She held it out toward Anne-Marie, but she simply shook her head. Both of them heard it ring and then a man's voice calling out Anne-Marie's name. Seeing her employee was going to squander this opportunity, Beatrice put the phone to her own ear. "This is Beatrice speaking. Is this Rich?"

"Yes, ma'am. Is Anne-Marie okay? Our call got disconnected."

"Yes, it's just this stupid phone."

"Oh, good. So, is Anne-Marie on her way then?"

"Right now? Oh, that would explain why she was in such a rush to leave. Yeah, she should be there in about twenty minutes. Have a blessed day." Beatrice hung up the phone and asked, "That wasn't too hard; now was it?"

"What have you done? I'm not going. He said this outfit was perfect for the interview." Anne-Marie plucked the bright pink fabric.

"Then I'd say he's got pretty good taste."

"Oh, Beatrice, I didn't mean any disrespect. It's just that you said the place was super fancy. I'd stick out like a sore thumb."

"I'm just messing with you. Come here. I've got just the thing for you to wear." Beatrice grabbed Anne-Marie's hand and pulled her through the office's back door and into her living space behind the shop.

Letting her go, Beatrice moved over to the closet and pulled out a cashmere sweater. "I bought this a while back, but I've never found the right time to wear it. I guess God wanted me to have it for your interview. Don't dawdle; get changed. Time's ticking, girl. You don't want to make them wait any longer than they already have."

Before Anne-Marie could form an argument, Beatrice had shoved her into the bathroom and shut the door. She could practically feel her boss breathing on the other side of the door, ready to spring into action if she took too long. Sighing,

Anne-Marie knew this was a losing battle. She'd humor Beatrice and then rub her nose in it when the employer at Kingston Air told her that she wasn't right for the job.

The sweater felt terrific, although it was a little snugger than she would have chosen for herself. Feeling slightly self-conscious at the curve-hugging fabric, she opened the door. "I don't know, Beatrice. Don't you think it's a little—"

"Perfect. You look stunning. Come on." Beatrice reached in and grabbed her hand once again. "I've never met anyone so reluctant to have a date with fate. Get your feet moving."

"Date with fate? Really, Beatrice?" Anne-Marie chuckled, but the butterflies in her stomach swarmed. She'd had the same thought earlier. Could it really be true?

Beatrice plucked her purse from the desk and locked the front door of the shop. "I'll just drive you to the place myself. That way, I'll know you actually went. I don't know what to do with young people these days. So scared of your own future."

"Beatrice, you don't have to drive me. I'm already putting you out. I'd feel really terrible if they offered me the job. Who would walk the brat pack?"

Beatrice threw her head back and laughed. "Is that what you call them? They're just sweet as pie with you. Besides, if you feel that bad about it, you can walk the little monsters on the weekend or after work. At least until I can train your replacement. How about that?"

"Oh, Beatrice. I can't stand the idea of not working with you every day. You're my only friend here in Houston."

"You're too sweet." Beatrice hummed along to the tunes on the radio as they drove through the heavy traffic.

Anne-Marie wondered if Beatrice had once been a cab driver with the way she skirted around traffic and took several side streets. By the time they pulled into the parking lot, Anne-Marie had no idea where they were.

Her nerves went on full alert as she saw the same logo outside the building, which had been stamped on the card. This was definitely the right place, even fancier than Beatrice had described. Way out of her league. She turned to face Beatrice, ready to beg her to take her back home.

"Get out, Anne-Marie. I'll be waiting right here until you're done."

"But—"

"Out!" Beatrice pointed and kept her expression stern.

"Yes, ma'am." Anne-Marie fumbled with the latch. "But I don't have a resume or anything."

"Out!"

Anne-Marie couldn't stop the erratic hammering of her heart. Standing outside the front door, she hesitated to open it. Could this really be her date with destiny? She looked over her shoulder to see Beatrice smiling encouragingly and giving her a thumb-up for her to go inside. She could do this for Beatrice.

CHAPTER 3
RICHARD

Richard watched the strange exchange from inside the lobby. With mirror finish glass tinting, he knew neither of them could see him. Unaccountably nervous, he took a deep breath in anticipation of Anne-Marie walking inside.

Only, she didn't open the door. She stood outside, seemingly frozen with indecision. What if she changed her mind and walked away? He needed her more than she could possibly know. Plus, he had a good feeling about her. After all, only good people could handle walking dogs for a living, right?

Taking action, Richard crossed the lobby and opened the door himself. Stepping outside, he waved at the older woman sitting in the car before turning to Anne-Marie. Signaling for her to enter before him, he said, "After you."

She woodenly stepped inside, not at all the graceful figure he'd admired when they first met. However, the cashmere sweater did look much better than her work uniform. It made him feel good that she cared enough about this interview to change into something nice—another sure sign he'd picked the right person for this job. Not that he would dare comment on her clothing, she'd probably bolt out the door.

He stepped ahead of her and opened another set of doors leading into the smallest conference room. This space only held five chairs rather than the usual fifteen. He didn't want to scare her by taking her back to his personal office. She seemed too much of a flight risk as it was.

"I hope you don't mind; I ordered some appetizers to munch on while we chat. I assume you're missing dinner because of me."

"Oh, that was nice of you. Thank you." Anne-Marie looked around as though she were trying to memorize the details. "This must be a lovely place to work. Will your boss be here soon?"

Shaking his head, he answered, "I'll be the one interviewing you."

Again, Anne-Marie's eyes narrowed suspiciously. "Why? I thought you were a mechanic or something." She took a moment to take in his outfit. "What do you do here?"

He watched her appraisal of his clothing, confident she could see the quality of his suit. His gym suit probably had given her the wrong idea about him. Richard chuckled and gestured for her to take a seat. As soon as she had settled, he unbuttoned the suit jacket and sat across from her. Rubbing above his eyebrow with his knuckle, he said, "I own this place. My name's Richard Kingston."

Seeing her eyes widen in surprise and her cheeks flush bright pink, he knew he'd embarrassed her. The silence stretched awkwardly between them. He pushed the appetizers closer to her and said, "Try the strawberries and scones. They're delicious."

Anne-Marie's hands clasped tighter together until her fingers turned white. Yet she didn't move or speak. Richard had to do or say something to repair the damage he'd caused.

"I suppose you're wondering why I asked you to fill this job."

Anne-Marie lifted her blue-eyed stare from her hands to his eyes. "Yes. We could start there. Then you could end by telling me why you didn't tell me the truth about who you really are."

The color of her sweater almost perfectly matched the hue of her neck and face. Richard picked up a scone and began pulling crumbs away from it to drop onto the appetizer plate in front of him. Why did she make him feel like an awkward teenager? Had he deceived her so blatantly?

"I didn't mean for you to get the wrong impression. I'm sorry if you felt like I'd tricked you in any way. It's really been a strange morning, and you caught me at an odd time. Besides, having a rottweiler's tongue as a napkin kind of threw me off my game." He'd struck a nerve with that comment. She couldn't look at him anymore.

Clearing her throat, she asked, "You said the last girl in this job wasn't qualified. Why did you hire her?"

"On paper, she looked perfect. In reality, she could hardly function. Too flighty. Too impulsive."

"Flighty? Seriously? No pun intended, right?"

Richard chuckled. She had a quick sense of humor, that was a positive trait in his books. "I actually didn't mean to, but it does describe her perfectly."

"Why did she leave?"

"She ran off with her new boyfriend. He promised her a sailing trip around the world, and she up and left without notice at lunch."

"Sounds familiar," Anne-Marie mumbled.

"What's that?" Richard popped the remnant of the scone in his mouth and chased it down with a swallow of water. Pushing the plate to the side and wiping away a few stray crumbs, he laced his fingers together and leaned forward.

"Nothing." She shook her head and almost whispered, "Why me?"

"Because you are kind, trustworthy, honest, and humble."

"And you know all of this because—"

"You walk dogs for a living."

Anne-Marie shook her head and started laughing. "You can't be serious. You assume all of those traits because I let a pack of dogs haul me all over the city?"

"I'm a firm believer that dogs are a good judge of character. Am I wrong about any of my assertions about you? Now's your chance to set the record straight."

Anne-Marie's expression softened. With her gaze once more lifting to meet his, she said, "I think we got off to a rough start. Can we start over?"

"Sure. You can start by telling me your full name and where you're from originally. You already know mine, and I've always lived in Houston."

"I'm Anne-Marie Pickler from Oregon. Nice to meet you, Richard."

"Any relation to the singer?"

"No, but I used to tell people I was so they wouldn't make fun of my name."

"Ah, so you do have a deviant streak. Noted." Richard grinned and waited for her to continue.

Anne-Marie's eyes widened until she realized he was only teasing.

"You said earlier that you're new to town. What brought you here?"

"I'd rather not say. I hope you don't mind."

"Not at all. Tell me about your work history?"

She spent the next few minutes sharing the string of odd jobs she'd had while attending college. Richard nodded in all of the right places, realizing she didn't have any administrative skills to speak of. Not that he cared. She'd finished college, and that spoke volumes to her desire to see things through.

"Where do you live now?" After hearing the address, Richard realized she was in the most run-down part of town, not too far from where he'd met her. More than ever, he wanted to help her, yet he had to worry about scaring her away. Something terrible had happened to her in the past, that much he could tell. From her reaction to the admission of his assistant running off, Richard assumed Anne-Marie's story might mirror that in some manner.

Not wanting to belabor the interview, Richard had already made up his mind. He wanted to help Anne-Marie, and he also wouldn't mind seeing her pretty face every day—not that he'd be sharing that tidbit with her. She reminded him of a lost puppy—one needing a safe place to stay. He could provide that for her, but he couldn't just come out and say that to her without sounding like a crazy stalker or something.

"Do you want a tour of the place? I'm sure you'd like to know a bit more about us before you decide to take the job I'm offering. Do you have any questions? I'm an open book."

"That's what you say now, but our history hasn't shown that to me all the time."

"Our history—that sounds like we have a chance for a future. I'll take it!" Richard stood, clapping his hands playfully, and said, "Let me show you around. I think you'll love everything."

Anne-Marie looked uncomfortable, her eyes darting back toward the conference room door. "I really shouldn't take up too much of your time. Plus, I have my ride waiting for me outside. Can I ask you one question, though?"

"Go for it." Richard leaned forward, with his fists resting on the tabletop. Trying to remain casual in the face of her interrogation, his muscles rippled under the sleeves of his jacket.

"Does this job come with a sign-on bonus?" She looked anywhere but at Richard.

He'd noticed her worn jeans and shabby sneakers earlier. He could well imagine she would need some money upfront to buy work clothes. Without hesitation, he said, "Absolutely. Does this mean you'll take the job?" Desperation dripped from his tone, yet he didn't even try to hide it. If he had to spend another day with Jimmy pestering him with the front office details, he'd probably quit himself.

His heart raced in anticipation as he watched Anne-Marie take her sweet time in answering. Finally, Richard sighed when he saw the slight nod of her head. "Great! I'll get that check for you. We can worry about the employment paperwork tomorrow morning. Wait, let me get your address again. I'll send a car to pick you up."

"No, I don't need that."

Richard thwacked his knuckles on the table, startling Anne-Marie into looking up. "No arguments. It's a perk of the job. Plus, having your own driver makes it so you can handle other details during your commute. It's a win-win, don't you think?"

"I guess."

"Your address?" Richard held out his phone and pulled up a blank contact page. "Ready when you are." He typed it in as she spoke. He really wanted to get her phone number, but he didn't want to press his luck. "Great. I'll be right back with your money."

Richard rushed from the room. He'd never given a sign-on bonus before, but he'd do just about anything to secure this opening with Anne-Marie. Reaching his desk in only a few seconds, he rummaged through his drawer to find the checkbook. Of course, it wasn't where he thought it was supposed to be. Anymore, he had the payroll department cut him a check, but they'd all gone home for the day.

Finally, he spotted the corner of the book poking out from under a stack of folders on the top of his desk. That seemed odd, but he didn't have time to ponder it. Ripping out the first check, he wrote down the first number that popped into his head. After scribbling an almost illegible signature, he raced out of his office and back to the conference room.

To find it empty. Whirling around, he hoped he'd just passed her waiting for him in the lobby. It was empty, as well. Glancing outside, he spotted her getting into the car she'd arrived in. "No! No, no. Don't leave again." He ran flat out across the lobby and flung the door open.

Like a maniac, he waved the check so she could see it and called out, "You forgot your bonus." He knew he looked the fool, but he could care less at this point—*better a fool than suffer from Jimmy's ineptitude.* Spotting the driver's side window open, he rushed to that side of the car and leaned against the sill.

"I'm glad I caught you. Here's the bonus I promised. I hope you'll find it satisfactory." Handing it to the driver's outstretched hand, Richard smiled and said. "You must be Anne-Marie's friend she was telling me about. I can't thank you enough for bringing her to the interview. My name's Richard Kingston."

"Beatrice Woolworth." She held out her hand and took his in a firm grasp. "The pleasure is all mine. You better treat Anne-Marie right—she's the best employee I've ever had. Honest to the day! You couldn't get any better."

"Those were my thoughts, as well. You must be the owner of Beatrice's Dog Walkers."

"The very same. Do you have a dog? I'll give you a 'friends and family' discount."

"Nope. No animals for me. I don't have enough free time to be fair to a pet."

"That's not right. You've got to reset your priorities if you can't take any time to enjoy life." She handed the check to Anne-Marie without even looking at it. She looked over to her passenger and asked, "Does that look right to you?"

Anne-Marie held the check as though it was burning her skin. Her eyes almost popped out of their sockets when she read the amount written. She thrust it back toward Richard, dangling it in front of Beatrice's face. "This is way too much. I'm sure that's not right. We don't have to worry about this right now. Please take it back."

Beatrice squinted to see the writing. Once she saw the amount, she began laughing. "Girl, get some common sense." She pushed Anne-Marie's hand away from her and started the engine of the car. "What time do you want her here tomorrow?" she asked Richard.

"I'm sending a car to pick her up." Richard leaned over further to make eye contact with Anne-Marie. "How does 7:30 sound to you?"

No answer came from the passenger side. Beatrice laughed again and answered, "Normally, I don't have any trouble getting her to talk. That sounds perfect. She'll be ready. Thank you, Mr. Kingston. You've been very kind to take such an interest in my Anne-Marie."

"Just Rich. Any friend of Anne-Marie's is a friend of mine. I hope you'll feel the same."

"Have a nice evening, Rich."

The car backed out of the spot right after Richard took a step back. He stood in the sweltering heat, watching the car leave the parking lot and down the road. More than anything, he wished he could be a fly on the wall in that car right now.

CHAPTER 4
ANNE-MARIE

"Have you gone and lost your mind, girl?" Beatrice asked just as they turned onto the road. "What do you mean trying to hand back that money? Don't you know how much that man is worth?"

"You must not have read that check right. He made it out for five thousand dollars! Five thousand!" Anne-Marie's gaze remained glued on the paper resting in her lap. She'd never seen so many zeros on a check before. Her bank probably wouldn't want to cash it.

"Pocket change, girl. Pocket change. Mr. Kingston is the town's most eligible billionaire. He won't miss it, but it definitely tells me he wants you to stick around. Too bad I wasn't walking your shift earlier today. That might have been me getting such a cushy job offer."

"Here, take it." Anne-Marie thrust the slip of paper toward Beatrice. "This whole thing makes me uncomfortable.

Things like this don't happen to girls like me. Besides, what strings are attached to this check? I really don't like it."

"Trust me; Mr. Kingston is the most upstanding man you'll ever find. They've written many articles about him in the local newspaper and international magazines. Not one bad word has been said about him. He's the real Mr. Nice Guy. Look, have I ever steered you wrong?" Beatrice took her eyes off of the road for a split second to look at her passenger. Taking pity on her, she added, "Not everyone is like Daniel. There are still some nice guys left in this world."

"I've been so wrong before. It's just easier not to take a chance." Anne-Marie admitted quietly.

"The only chance you'll be taking with Rich is whether or not he'll think you look hot in the new wardrobe we're about to buy for you."

"Beatrice!"

Her friend didn't respond with anything but another outburst of laughter. They ended up going to Beatrice's bank, where she convinced the bank manager to cash the check with the guarantee of funds from her business bank account.

If she felt uncomfortable walking in with such a large amount, she felt doubly so with the knowledge she had stacks of hundred dollar bills in her purse. Clutching the small bag tightly to her side, her eyes darted from side to side, looking for would-be robbers.

"Calm down, girl. You look like you just robbed a bank."

"I feel like I did. Let's hurry and spend this before someone comes and takes it from me."

Beatrice laughed again. "Would you like me to carry your purse? I honestly wouldn't mind."

"Gladly!" Anne-Marie pushed it toward her and instantly grabbed Beatrice's in its place. Settling the strap on her shoulder, she sighed, and some of the tension left her body.

By the time they made it back to her shabby apartment, Anne-Marie wanted to wilt onto her disgusting sofa and rub her sore feet. Who knew Beatrice had so much energy to shop until she dropped? She guessed it was easier to spend someone else's money, but she still had over fifteen hundred dollars in her purse.

Pulling the bank envelope out, she tucked it into the ripped seam on her couch cushion. It was probably the first place a burglar would look, but it was the best she could think of right now. Bags of clothes and shoes surrounded her, and she'd never felt so lonely in all of her life. Beatrice had wished her luck tomorrow, but she felt like luck wasn't going to be nearly enough. She needed experience if she wasn't going to make a complete fool out of herself.

I wonder if Rich will tell me how awful I am at the job. Or, will he simply shake his head and walk away, too disgusted to correct me? What have I gotten myself into?

Anne-Marie left the mess in the living room and took a long, hot shower. Morning would be here before she knew it, and she needed to clear her head and relax for a few minutes. By the time she was ready for bed, she had her outfit laid out, her breakfast bar sitting on the counter, and her two alarms set right next to her bed.

All she had to do was sleep. Morning would come way too soon. Yet sleep refused to come for her. If only she could call her mom and get her advice. What would she tell her? How would her mom react? Anne-Marie didn't want to find out; she was too chicken.

Sleep must have happened since the alarm beeped annoyingly next to her head. Feeling groggy, she slapped the alarm until it shut up, but the other one was out of reach. She had to get out of bed to turn that one off. Too many times, she'd shut off her alarms while she was sleeping. Today was not going to be that day.

Another shower helped to wake her, but it didn't do anything for the dark circles under her eyes. She didn't even have the right makeup to hide it entirely. Disgusted, she spent extra time on her hair and hoped Rich wouldn't notice.

Rechecking the time, probably the fortieth glance in the last five minutes, she hurried to get dressed. With a peek down onto the street, she spotted a fancy car turning the corner and heading toward her place. It had to be for her considering she'd never before seen anything nearly as snazzy in this neighborhood.

Grabbing her purse from the dining table, she rushed out to meet it before it could draw too much attention. She sped down the two flights of stairs faster than was probably advisable in high heels. On the last step, she felt her ankle twist, but she didn't have time to contemplate it. Bursting through the lobby door, she arrived out of breath just in time for the driver to walk around the front of the car to open her door.

"Miss Pickler?"

"Yes. Thank you. And what's your name?" She waited with her hands resting on the top of the door and faced the chauffeur.

"Wilson, ma'am. I'll be your permanent driver. If you need anything, please let me know. Here's my card."

Anne-Marie took the paper and slipped it into her purse. With a friendly nod, she sank into the back seat. With a solid thud, the door shut, and she watched Wilson walk around the car and resume his place behind the steering wheel. The black car pulled away from the curb, and soundlessly entered the morning traffic.

"Wilson? How long have you been working for Mr. Kingston?" Anne-Marie scooted to the edge of the seat and leaned against the center console.

"I'd say about eight years, Miss. Pickler."

"Please just call me Anne-Marie. It makes me feel so old to have you address me so formally."

"As you wish, Miss Anne-Marie."

"Were you assigned to drive the last executive assistant?"

"No, ma'am."

"Why not?"

"Her boyfriend insisted on driving her himself."

"Ah." Anne-Marie only hesitated a second before she rushed to ask the question burning on her tongue. "Is Mr. Kingston a nice man, or should I be on guard?"

"Oh, Miss Anne-Marie, he's the nicest person you'll ever meet. You'll never have to worry when he's around. He's honest to a fault and a straight-shooter. You never have to guess what he's thinking; he'll tell you himself."

"Everyone keeps saying that," Anne-Marie murmured.

"Then, you best start believing it." Wilson nodded matter-of-factly. He winked at her in the rear-view mirror before he smiled once again.

Anne-Marie sat back and crossed her arms. Maybe God was trying to help her, after all. She closed her eyes and said a quick prayer. "Please, Lord, watch over me today and help me not make a fool of myself." Maybe her mother's dire prediction that this was the devil's errand that she would run off to chase a cowboy had been wrong. Perhaps this was precisely what she needed to find the life she was meant to live.

Before she knew it, the car stopped outside the main doors to the Kingston Air headquarters. Wilson opened her door and gave her a curt bow before returning to the driver's seat. "Just give me a jingle when you're ready to leave. I'm at your service all day, every day."

"Thank you, Wilson. You've been so kind." She only took two steps across the sidewalk before she realized how painful her ankle felt. Her leg buckled under her, and she would have fallen had Richard not appeared seemingly from out of nowhere.

"Hey, are you okay?" he asked, his arm solidly around her waist.

"I twisted my ankle racing down the stairs to meet the car." Anne-Marie winced as she tried to put some weight on her foot again.

"Well, we can't have that." Without any warning, Richard swung her up into his arms and carried her into the building.

Anne-Marie's complexion turned rose pink as she clung to Richard's rock-hard shoulders. This only happened in the movies, not to girls like her. She had to keep reminding herself to hold still; she hated it when the girls in films struggled. Besides, she didn't want to cause Richard to drop her; that would be even more mortifying.

"Sounds like someone was eager to get to work. So much so, you injured yourself. Let's take a look at this, shall we?" Richard set her down on the couch and kneeled in front of her.

With incredibly gentle hands, he removed her shoe while supporting her stockinged foot. "Looks a tad bit swollen. Stay here while I get you an ice pack from the first-aid kit."

Anne-Marie could hardly argue. After all, she'd fallen into his arms. Embarrassing for sure, but not the worst thing to happen in her lifetime. Getting caught skinny-dipping by her best friend's boyfriend totally outshined this little incident. Still, she hoped none of the employees would find her like this.

As if her thoughts had caused people to materialize, the lobby door opened, and several people walked in. They obviously knew one another well as they joked and spoke loudly with one another. All sound stopped as one of them spotted her and elbowed the others to get their attention. Instead of continuing through the lobby, they turned to head toward her.

"Can I help you?" the first man asked.

"Ah, Jimmy! I see you've met my new executive assistant. Anne-Marie, this is Jimmy, Andrew, and Ed. They are my top salesmen." Richard dropped back to Anne-Marie's foot and gently placed the ice pack in place. "How's that?"

"It's good. Thank you." Anne-Marie shifted her gaze from Richard up to the three employees. "It's nice to meet you."

"Likewise," Jimmy said. "We should get to work, guys."

They grinned at one another before heading to the back of the lobby, presumably to their offices.

Anne-Marie leaned forward and whispered, "Was that the guy you wanted me to replace?"

Richard dropped back onto his heels and laughed. "The one and the same. Great salesman, terrible assistant."

"Hey! I heard that!" Jimmy yelled across the lobby.

"You know it's true, man!" Richard shot back.

Sounds of unrestrained laughter answered him, and he returned his attention to Anne-Marie. "I guess I can bring all of the employment paperwork to you here while that ice does its job. I'll be right back."

Not the most auspicious of beginnings, but Anne-Marie knew how to roll with the punches. She took this time alone to look around. Beatrice had peppered her with questions she couldn't answer, and she promised to do better next time.

Richard returned with a folder, a small packet, and bottled water. He moved to sit beside her on the oversized couch. "I thought you could use some pain killers while we go over your paperwork." He handed her a pen and the folder after she took the medication. "I'll leave you to this for about twenty minutes; then I'll come back. Don't try to walk before then, okay?"

Anne-Marie marveled at how Richard seemed to know exactly how to handle her strange situation. How many invalids had he employed before? When she had all of the paperwork squared away, Richard showed up with one more surprise. A wheelchair.

"Do you have those just sitting around?" Anne-Marie couldn't help but laugh, although it came out sounding slightly forced.

"No, I sent Wilson out to get it. I hope you don't mind. I wanted to give you a tour, and this seemed like the safest way to get it done."

Ah, yes. Wilson would have had a front-row seat to her spectacular display of clumsiness. At least now he knew what to expect from her in the future. "Well, since you've gone to all the trouble, it would be pretty rude of me to refuse." She didn't want to tell Richard about how much practice she'd had in a wheelchair as an accident-prone teenager.

"Perfect! Your chariot awaits!" Richard rolled the chair right next to the couch and hovered while Anne-Marie almost-gracefully transferred herself to the thick cushioned seat. "Are you ready?"

None of the chairs her parents had rented or borrowed had ever been half as plush as this one. She should have known he'd only get the best, even for lowly employees such as herself. "Yep. I'm ready to be amazed!"

Richard chuckled and grabbed the handles at the back of the chair. As they rolled through the vast building, Anne-Marie could hear the pride of ownership in Richard's voice. Aviation was his passion, and it showed in the craftsmanship of the different aircraft styles waiting in the showroom hangar. No detail was left untouched.

Beatrice had been right that these aircraft were only for the ultra-wealthy population. She couldn't even imagine what the maintenance costs would be, let alone the acquisition price.

"It's funny that I ended up working here," Anne-Marie said when they finished the tour at the small deli outside of the client appreciation lobby. She'd spent so many afternoons with her father in little restaurants beside the airstrips where they'd landed. Warm, nearly forgotten memories flooded through her.

"Oh, yeah? Why is that?"

"My dad was in the Airforce, and he was a private pilot."

"That's cool. We'll have to invite him over for a tour."

"He died two years ago. Complications from Parkinson's." Anne-Marie added the final details to end the conversation before she thought about it long enough to cry. Nobody really understood Parkinson's the way the families did. It was an easy way to keep people from prying.

"I'm sorry."

Offhandedly waving her hand to dismiss his apology, she continued, "Anyway, I used to go flying with him. He even let me take the controls once we were in the air. I loved my special time alone with him. You know, I always meant to get my pilot's license, but it was so expensive. At least now, I get to be around airplanes that I'm certain my dad would have loved."

"Do you still want to learn to fly?" Richard's gaze never left the airfield outside.

Anne-Marie's eyes flicked over to his face, but he wasn't looking at her. Deciding he was just making small talk, she answered honestly, "Someday. Maybe. I don't know. It's pretty low on my priorities list these days."

"What's at the top of the list?" This time, Richard did look at her. Intently.

A nervous chuckle escaped her lips, and she blurted, "Paying rent. Maybe finding a better neighborhood to live in. Food. Things like that. You know, life's essentials."

CHAPTER 5

RICHARD

R ichard winced at her list of 'essentials.' Those were things he seldom even considered. He'd grown up with wealth, made his fortune away from the family business, and never had to worry about things like a safe place to live.

He hated thinking that Anne-Marie had to deal with those concerns. She had such a big heart, too kind for her own good. More than ever, he wanted to do something to help her out. Asking her to take this job had been more of a blessing than he initially realized—both for himself and her. It also made him feel guilty for only considering his needs, not once realizing he would be changing her life with his simple, selfish offer.

He would make amends for his thoughtlessness; it was the least he could do. "We never did discuss the salary for your job. Do you realize that?"

A flush blossomed across her cheeks, making her blue eyes sparkle brighter in contrast. "I guess not. Although I don't expect much after that ridiculous check you gave me. I figured that should just about cover the first six months of my wages."

Richard shook his head, his eyes danced with mirth, and his shoulders shook as he silently laughed. Was this girl for real? Did she not understand the position she'd accepted? Apparently not. "Do you want me to tell you, or do you want to be surprised when you get your first paycheck in two weeks?"

"Might as well rip the bandage off right now. Hit me with it." She leveled her gaze at him and waited.

He had her full attention now. "It's eight thousand a month, plus benefits." He expected her to be pleased, but that's not at all how she reacted.

Red splotches immediately replaced the rosiness on her cheeks, and her hands gripped the armrests of the wheelchair until her fingers turned white. Leaning forward, she spat out the words, "Are you kidding me?"

Slightly confused, Richard blurted, "Is that not enough? I suppose I could raise it to ten grand if that would make you happier." He'd double her salary without giving it a second thought, but he doubted she'd agree to it.

Anne-Marie sputtered, but she couldn't seem to get the words to come out of her mouth. Instead, she shook her head before she finally replied, "Eight grand is ridiculous! I'm not a charity case for you to take on. I won't stand for it. You're going to pay me a reasonable rate and not one penny over. Good grief, I don't even have any experience, and you're planning on paying me top dollar. I won't take it."

Richard resisted laughing, knowing it would only anger her more. Instead, he sighed and slowly shook his head. He'd have to take a new angle before she'd be convinced of his sincerity.

"Wow, you are really a tough nut to crack. C'mon. I'm going to introduce you to the payroll manager. I'm pretty sure you won't be so mad at me once you finish talking with him." He sprang to his feet and moved to take the handles of the wheelchair once again. At least behind her, he could let the grin escape unnoticed.

She remained stock-still in the chair, her hands never releasing their death grip. She seemed to have found her tongue. "What are you going on about? Why would the payroll manager make me think any differently about this?"

If she wanted the bald truth, then he'd give it to her straight. "Because you have no idea what you're talking about. Just wait. Ask Paul how much Brandy made when she started."

"How much was it?" Anne-Marie twisted around until she could see his face.

Seeing her beginning to turn, he altered his expression to neutrality. Richard mimed zipping his lips shut and kept walking. When Anne-Marie turned back around in a huff, he almost lost control of the delight, which threatened to explode from him. Knocking on Paul's door, he said, "I'm going to leave Anne-Marie with you to talk about employee wages. Feel free to answer any questions she asks."

Paul's eyebrows rose, but he nodded cordially. "You got it, Rich."

Richard walked around the corner, purposefully leaving the office door open so he could eavesdrop on the conversation. Sure enough, Anne-Marie led by asking about Brandy's salary. He only waited for a couple of minutes before returning.

He wheeled her back the way they'd come. He figured she'd had enough time to digest Paul's confirmation of her salary. Acting as if he hadn't heard every word they discussed, he asked, "Did you find out everything you needed to know?"

Anne-Marie's gaze dropped to her lap. She nodded. "Yes. I'm sorry, Mr. Kingston. I spoke out of turn."

She must be feeling contrite to become so formal with him suddenly. That wasn't going to work. He stopped so abruptly, her whole body shook. He stepped around her chair and kneeled in front of her. Luckily, they were alone in the hallway—he didn't want to reprimand her with an audience. "We need to get one thing straight." He purposely left his tone sharp so she'd pay attention.

Anne-Marie wouldn't meet his gaze. He could barely hear her reply. "What's that?"

He wanted to reach out and touch her chin, but he kept his hands to himself. "No more, 'Mr. Kingston,' unless I'm meeting with a client. You are to call me Rich or Richard. I'll leave which one up to you. We're a family here." Taking pity on her, he softened his tone. "Formality has its place, but not when we're alone. Can we agree to that?"

Her gaze flicked over to meet his. Barely above a whisper, she said, "Yes, Rich. I can work with that."

Playfulness returned to his expression, and his lips pulled back into a smile wide enough to show his molars. "Great. Now, I've saved our offices for last on our tour. Are you ready to see where you'll spend a third of your life?"

Some of her normal light returned to her eyes, and her tone had some playfulness back. "Wow, that sounds ominous. Although, if it looks anything like the rest of your headquarters, then it'll be a definite improvement over my dumpy apartment. I'm ready to be dazzled."

"Your wish is my command." Richard wished he had more time to get her acquainted with her new duties, but a glance at his watch reminded him that he only had a few more minutes to devote to her before his next meeting.

Crossing the lobby, he turned to the private elevator and punched the button. "Our offices are on the second floor. I think you'll like the view." Only seconds after they entered the lift, the doors opened to the executive suite.

The thrill of seeing it from Anne-Marie's perspective made him giddy all over again. Just like the first time he walked into this space, his eyes took in the plush leather furniture, the thick Berber carpet, and the panoramic view of the parked airplanes and the airstrip outside the wall of windows. Even after eight years, he wouldn't change a thing about it.

When Anne-Marie remained silent, Richard couldn't. "Well. What do you think? Can you manage to work here?"

"It might be a struggle," Anne-Marie choked out.

Richard looked down at the top of her head, wishing he could see her face to find out what she meant. Seeing her head shake slowly, he hoped she wouldn't change her mind and decide to quit already. "What's wrong with it?"

This time, Anne-Marie twisted around until she could look up at him. Casting her hand out in a broad arc to indicate the entirety of the space, she said, "It's too perfect. I mean, what if I spill coffee or accidentally drop the toner cartridge on the carpet?"

Richard instantly relaxed and let the laughter escape from him. Now that he knew she was adequately impressed, he could address her misgivings. He clicked his tongue at her, unable to resist asking, "Are you always this practical?"

"I'm a realist!"

"Fine, then I'll answer your concerns with reality. We have a nightly cleaning crew and a maintenance contract for the copy machines, so you'll never have to worry about mucking around inside the equipment. Does that alleviate your concerns?" He took her silence as agreement.

He wheeled her chair into his office and received the proper praise for the stately appearance before he ended the tour at her desk. "And this is where you'll spend the majority of your time."

Outside, he spotted a jet rolling to a stop at the FBO entrance. Another glance at his watch let him know he had only a couple more minutes. Pointing outside, Richard said, "That's my next appointment. We're working on a partnership with his tug company. You'll find all of his company's information inside this folder." Richard tapped the file on the desktop. "I'm sorry I won't be able to spend much more time with you today, but I want you to look through everything, familiarize yourself with where things are."

"You mean you want me to snoop?" Anne-Marie's face scrunched up with distaste.

"Call it what you want, but this is your domain now. I want you to think of it as your home away from home. You have another folder that details your duties and the schedule for when to get things done. If you have any questions, feel free to ask. I have an open-door policy."

Pointing to his left, he said, "There's a stocked fridge over there. Feel free to eat whatever you want in here, or you can go back to the deli downstairs. Everything is free for employees. If you can't find something you like, ask Wilson to pick something up or have him take you out for lunch. You get one hour to eat and can take it at any time between eleven and one."

Digging inside his coat pocket, he produced a black credit card, which he placed on the desk next to the folder. "This is for your work expenses, including lunch, should you choose to eat off-site."

The elevator doors opened. George Hansen's gaze first met Richard's before it passed down to Anne-Marie's. His demeanor instantly changed, which Richard recognized and didn't like one little bit.

"And who is this lovely lady?" George smoothly asked once he crossed the room. He may have been asking Richard, but like a snake ready to strike, his eyes never left Anne-Marie.

"This is Anne-Marie Pickler, my new executive assistant. Anne-Marie, this is George Hansen from Smart Tug Systems. I have everything ready for us inside my office, George."

George winked at Anne-Marie before he finally turned his full attention to Richard. "What happened with the lovely Brandy?"

"She wanted an adventure on the high seas. Shall we?" Richard didn't want to discuss his employees with George, but if it kept him from staring at his new employee, then he'd put up with it a little longer. Gesturing for them to enter his office, he didn't leave George much choice but to go.

# CHAPTER 6
ANNE-MARIE

Anne-Marie seldom had a hard time speaking up for herself. For some reason, ever since she'd run into Richard, she'd found herself at a loss for words. If only she could have Beatrice working with her here, then she'd feel right at home. As it was, she'd have to find some way to get used to all of this luxury surrounding her.

For sure, her cheeks were pink, a condition that had long since stopped troubling her. She could not be responsible for her unconscious reaction because of her unusually pale skin. Not since Daniel had a man looked at her so intently. Yet, the fluttering inside her stomach made her feel alive.

George Hansen was nothing like Daniel. This man was successful and wealthy. Daniel had been a poor mechanic with only his good looks to get him by in life. George's classical features, well-built body, and tailored clothes made

Daniel look like a garbageman in comparison. And he'd flirted with her shamelessly.

It took several minutes of daydreaming before the phone ringing brought her back to reality. She picked up the receiver and managed to spit out a semi-professional greeting to the caller. Luckily, it was a spam caller for computer repair. She hung up with a sigh of relief. She had to get herself together if only to be partially worthy of the ridiculous pay this job offered.

She could hardly wait to get off of work and tell Beatrice all about it.

Focus!

Looking down at the desk, she spotted the black card Richard had left. Picking it up, she saw her name printed on the front.

How in the world had Richard gotten this personalized card so fast?

She'd heard about black cards before. No spending limit. Why in the world would Richard entrust her with this before he even knew her?

Shaking her head and drawing in a shaky breath, Anne-Marie tucked the card inside her purse. Hopefully, she'd never need to use it. But it did give her a giddy feeling knowing that she could pay for lunch, mostly since she hadn't thought to pack one.

Her eyes traveled over to the wet bar across from her. Deciding to test out her ankle in the relative privacy of her office, she stood and took a tentative step. The medication must have kicked in since she only felt stiff but not sore. Feeling bold, she walked across the room and bent over to investigate the contents of the refrigerator.

A hand touching the small of her back had her squealing with fright, straightening up, and whirling around. Pain radiated through her ankle as it twisted again.

"Sorry to startle you. I came to get some water. Do you mind?" George innocently held his hands out in front of him, his eyes sparkling with delight.

Why was she so jumpy? It wasn't as if he'd grabbed her rear, which would have been just as easy. She felt foolish for overreacting. "Oh, sorry. Yes. Help yourself." Anne-Marie grabbed the counter to steady her as she moved out of the way. "I didn't hear you come up behind me."

"I gathered that. But since we have a minute alone, I was wondering if you were free for dinner tonight. I'm only in town for a few hours and would love to have some beautiful company."

Her heart hammered in her chest, and it suddenly felt hot in the room. "Um. Sure." Why did she agree so readily? She sounded desperate, even to herself.

"Great. I'll get a car and pick you up at five. How does that sound?" George twisted the top off of the bottle and took a swig of water. His tongue darted out to catch the drip quivering from his upper lip.

Anne-Marie couldn't stop staring at his perfect, sensual lips surrounded by just the right amount of sexy scruff. She'd always been a sucker for the unshaven look. George could have been a poster model for it. Clearing her throat, she said, "Um, I've already got a car. You won't need to get one." Plus, she'd rather not be alone with a stranger. At least Wilson would know where she'd gone and with whom.

"Even better. Once Richard and I finish our meeting, I'll be ready to go. See you in a few hours." Another wink, and he turned to go.

Anne-Marie stared after his perfect posture and sexy swagger. This man exuded confidence. He knew exactly what to say to make her feel special. Yet alarm bells kept firing inside her mind, which she immediately brushed aside like an unwanted noise. She needed a distraction.

Why not let George take her out for a night on the town? It wasn't like she'd had an opportunity to do so since arriving. She'd merely stayed in survival mode.

Limping back to her desk, she found the first-aid kit inside the bottom drawer. Rummaging through it, she found more pain killers and ate them dry since she'd forgotten to get a water bottle. She scrunched up her nose at the bitterness of the aspirin. It was too much trouble to try to get back there, and she refused to use the wheelchair in case George popped back out of Richard's office again.

She opened the folder on George's business and began reading through it. Smart Tug Systems appeared to be a very lucrative company and an excellent fit for merging with Richard's. The uneasiness she felt in George's presence evaporated as she realized he was a very wealthy man who simply didn't want to spend dinner alone.

She could understand that feeling. The sofa in her apartment could attest to the countless nights eating take-out pizza alone with only the television for company. She would gladly be the distraction George needed. It would only be better if Daniel happened to spot her out on the town with another guy. Then he'd realize what he'd missed out on.

Anne-Marie chuckled. Her thoughts sounded more like her crazy high-school girlfriend who liked to string guys along and let them fight over her attention. That wasn't like Anne-Marie at all. She was a one-partner person. Not that that had worked out all that well for her, either.

The afternoon flew by. She'd read through every file in Brandy's desk and even threw out some love notes she'd found tucked in the back of one of the drawers. It was no wonder Brandy had been so flaky at work; she was too busy flirting to get anything done.

Richard and George left Richard's office together, both of them laughing at some unknown comment. George made a beeline to Anne-Marie's desk and asked, "Are you ready to go?"

"What's this?" Richard asked; his tone sounded pleasant, but the muscles along his jawline tightened perceptibly. "Do you two know one another?"

Anne-Marie grabbed her purse and stood. She didn't want to cause any tension, but she could see George's attention bothered Richard. "George didn't want to have dinner alone. You could join us if you like."

Please say, no!

"Ah, no. Another time maybe. I've got some calls I need to make and dinner plans of my own. George," he held out his hand and grasped George's a little too hard, "I'm glad we're going to get this deal put together. I think we'll both make a killing on it. I'll see you next week." With that said, he turned smartly on his heel and returned to his office. The door closed just short of a slam.

Anne-Marie winced, thinking she'd already made a grave mistake. She did not want Richard mad at her. With only the two of them in the office, it could potentially be very awkward.

"After you," George said.

Her eyes darted from the closed office door to George. A smile flittered across her lips, but it didn't reach her eyes. "Of course. You must be starving. Are you familiar with the restaurants around here?"

"Yes. Very. I know just the place we should go."

"Oh, good. I'm new to town. If you didn't, then I was going to ask my driver to take us somewhere nice."

"Your driver?"

"Yes. Company car and all." Anne-Marie surprised herself with how quickly she adjusted to the perks of her job. Surely the novelty would wear off soon, but right now, it felt pretty special. She managed to walk gracefully to the elevator and across the front lobby. Luckily, Wilson had parked directly outside the front entrance and held the door open for her. "I hope you don't mind taking us out to dinner, Wilson."

Wilson nodded curtly. "Not a problem, Miss. Anne-Marie. Where to?"

Anne-Marie looked behind her before answering. "Mr. Hansen will let you know." She ducked into the car and scooted across the back seat without hearing where they would go. Tugging at the hem of her skirt, she wished she'd worn pants since so much of her thighs were exposed. Yet, she only planned to be sitting hidden behind a desk, not having dinner dates with sexy strangers.

George sat next to her, and the door closed behind him with a solid thud. The sound matched that of her heart beating wildly. Never in a million years would she have thought her evening would end like this.

"So, Anne-Marie, what's your story?" George casually dropped his hand on her knee and gave it a gentle squeeze.

Anne-Marie's mouth suddenly went dry, as though she'd chewed a dozen aspirin tablets all at once. Only the sheer material of her pantyhose stood between her flesh and his warmth. No worries over him snagging the delicate fabric, the smoothness of his skin bespoke of enough money to pay people to do any hard labor he required.

She couldn't stop staring at his hand or what he meant by touching her. With remarkable speed, she plucked his hand away from her flesh and dropped it on the seat beside her. "Not that."

"I'm sorry. I didn't mean to imply anything improper." George scooted aside and shifted, so his back rested against the door, and his knee propped up on the seat between them. "Is that better?"

"Yes. Thank you. I'm sorry if I overreacted."

"Don't be. I should learn to keep my hands to myself. My mother tried and tried to instill that in me, but I never listened." George grinned playfully, but it reminded Anne-Marie of a wolf playing with a sheep. "I hope you like Italian food. There's this great place on the penthouse. The view is almost as stunning as you are."

"Quite the charmer, aren't you?" Anne-Marie lifted her brow and looked up to see Wilson eyeing them in the rear-view mirror. She nodded minutely, hoping Wilson would understand that she was glad to have him as a chaperone.

They entered the restaurant ten minutes later. Just as George had promised, the view took her breath away. She'd only ever seen places like this on Lifestyles of the Rich and Famous. The hostess led them to a table right next to the window.

George held out the chair and waited for her to be seated. Anne-Marie looked down and down to the street twenty-three stories below. "It's a good thing I'm not afraid of heights."

Pointing, George leaned over Anne-Marie until his chest rested on her shoulder. "You can see the Kingston airfield just over there."

Woodsy musk-scented cologne assailed Anne-Marie's senses, almost making her dizzy as she inhaled it. She'd smelled this scent before, but she couldn't readily place it. "You're right. I bet the view gets better once it's dark outside."

"Like I said, stunning," George murmured close to her ear. His gaze no longer looked out the window.

Anne-Marie stiffened as she realized he probably had a clear view down the front of her shirt. She grabbed up her napkin, and jerkily shifted her body away from George. He must have gotten the message loud and clear since he straightened and casually took his place across from her.

He didn't even seem fazed; he looked as relaxed and comfortable as ever with his smug expression. Leaning against the back of his chair, he picked up the one-page menu and spoke of the night's specials.

Anne-Marie didn't remember what she ordered; she really just wanted the evening over. When her phone began ringing in her purse, she almost jumped out of her chair to answer it. She should have remembered to silence the ringer before coming into the fancy restaurant. "Do you mind if I take this call?" she asked, raising her eyebrows toward George.

"Not at all. I'll just enjoy the view."

He never took his eyes off of her as she swiped the screen. "Hi, Beatrice. Yeah, I'm sorry I didn't call you when I got off of work. I'm actually at Venci's with a client. Can I call you back when I get home tonight? You're a doll. Love you, too."

She hung up and then silenced the phone before dropping it back in her purse. "I'm so sorry. She's my best friend and wanted to find out how my first day at the office went."

"First day, huh? I'm glad to celebrate this momentous occasion with you. How about we have a toast to new beginnings?" He held up his glass of red wine.

She'd refused the wine and held up her glass of water. Feeling foolish, she clinked her glass with his and swiftly took a sip. More than anything, she yearned to relax on her old, worn couch.

Then, the unexpected happened. Richard walked in with a beautiful woman clinging to his arm. He hadn't seen them; he only had eyes for his date. Her heart lurched, and she lost her appetite.

"Do you want to dance?" George asked.

"Sure," she automatically answered.

George stood and held out his hand. She took it, grateful for the help. She should have taken more pain killers before leaving the office. At this rate, she'd be stuck using Richard's wheelchair permanently. George led her onto the small dancefloor, where the slow music played softly in the background.

He pulled her body close to his and wrapped his arms around her. She put her arms around his neck and used his strength to support her weak ankle.

CHAPTER 7
RICHARD

Richard could only see red as his office door slammed behind him. Which was utterly unreasonable considering Anne-Marie was his employee. He didn't have any say in what she did with her free time. But having her meet George and immediately agree to dinner with him angered him beyond belief.

The idea of spending the evening alone no longer sounded appealing. Deciding to do something he swore not to do again, he opened the dating app on the cell phone and swiped the first girl's picture who caught his attention. Not wanting to make small talk, he sent her a message. "Dinner tonight?"

As if she'd been staring at the phone, desperate for attention, she immediately responded. "Absolutely. What time?"

"Now. Meet me at Venci's?"

"I can be there in twenty minutes. You?"

"Same. My name's Richard."

"Veronica. See you soon! "

Ugh, did she really just use an emoji? This was probably a big mistake. But if he didn't show up, then he'd feel like a bigger schmuck. Hopefully, she would have something interesting to talk about. He didn't think he could handle another evening of insipid conversation like the last time he'd used this app.

Richard let the valet take his car. He purposely arrived ten minutes early so Veronica wouldn't see his car. The last thing he needed was another clingy girl, only after his assets. He glanced at his Rolex. In another two minutes, she'd be late. He hated tardiness almost as much as he hated waiting for people. His father had always insisted on punctuality, and Richard had to agree with him on this one point. Anything less than punctual signaled disrespect.

With a minute to spare, Veronica's cab pulled in front of the restaurant. Richard stepped forward and opened the car door for her. "Right on time. It's nice to meet you, Veronica."

Turning her blue eyes up to his, she sighed with pleasure when she looked at him. She practically gushed, breathlessly, "The pleasure is all mine, Richard." Her fingers curled around his forearm, and she stepped close to his side.

Already, Richard felt smothered, like Veronica was attempting to be a second skin on him. It was a bad fit. This was a mistake, but he'd endure it for the evening. If nothing else, he could give this woman an unforgettable dining experience to share with her girlfriends.

Forcing himself to make small talk, he asked, "Have you eaten here before?"

Veronica shook her head, inhaling deeply before answering. "Never. I've heard good things about it, though. Have you tried it?"

He turned his head away from the reek of cigarette smoke still on her breath. "Yes. It's a favorite of mine." It might become his least favorite if things got any worse.

She squeezed even closer to his side if that were possible. "Oh, good. You can order something for me. I don't speak Italian."

Ugh. Now, he'd have to figure out if she was a salad girl or someone who actually ate. That meant he'd have to discuss her dietary habits—another sure warning to a doomed evening.

If only Anne-Marie could be the woman with him, then he could relax and enjoy her company. But this wasn't Anne-Marie, nor would it ever be. She clearly didn't have any interest in him, and he'd be well-advised not to show any interest in her. She was an employee. Nothing more.

The hostess walked them across the dining room. Richard's gaze immediately fell on Anne-Marie and George making a toast. To what, he could only guess.

He should have known George would take her out to the most expensive restaurant in the city for a first date. That was the kind of guy George was—flashy, outgoing, and overconfident. But Anne-Marie looked like she was having a spectacular time. They even stood and went to the dance floor.

He wanted to have her body held close to his. He wanted to have her arms wrapped around his neck again like they'd been this morning when he'd carried her petite frame into the lobby. Why was he having these unsolicited thoughts? Anne-Marie was off-limits. And she was taken. By George, of all people.

His gut twisted with jealousy—a sensation he hadn't experienced since high school when the girl he wanted to ask to prom picked the football team captain instead of him. He thought he'd outgrown such juvenile feelings—apparently not.

"Is that someone you know?" Veronica asked, her voice high and soft next to his ear.

"Yeah. She's my executive assistant, and he's my new business partner." The words sounded bitter and hollow as they came out. He didn't care.

"Do you want to go over and say hello? I don't mind."

If he said anything to them, it wouldn't be polite. Better if he steered clear. "No. They're on a date. I don't want to disturb them. Besides, that would be terribly rude of me."

That seemed to be the right thing to say. Veronica squeezed his arm tighter, and she actually sighed. "I hope you don't mind if I only eat something light tonight. I had a late lunch."

Richard held out her chair, then seated himself. Picking up the menu, he asked, "Does a feta salad sound too filling?"

"No, that sounds dreamy. Thank you for taking such good care of me. It really is nice when a man can take charge. I bet you get that a lot, though. You're so distinguished and polished. What do you do for a living?"

And there it was, the pickup line he'd heard too many times to count. Deciding to fall back on the answer his brother used, he replied, "I work with numbers. Do you like accounting?"

Veronica laughed, shrill, and prolonged. "You're too funny! The only numbers I like are on my credit card."

Of course. Classic gold-digger answer. "Do you work?" Richard just had to ask, even though he knew the answer already.

"Only when I have to. My grandmama left me a bit of money when she died. I usually only pick up odd jobs when the fancy strikes me."

"I could help you invest that money if you're interested, that is." Richard couldn't resist the bait. He knew she was lying by how she twirled the curl in her hair and refused to make eye contact with him. She didn't have two dimes to rub together, which was why she was on the dating app.

It actually surprised him that she didn't want to order the biggest meal on the menu so that she'd have leftovers to take home. He'd had that kind of date before.

Another shrill laugh punctuated the silence. "Nah, my pappy handles all that. You don't need to worry about me. But tell me more about your job. It sounds fascinating."

Richard extolled her with all of Charles's stultifying stories of tax refunds, funds diversions, and investments. It actually surprised Richard how many of the stories he remembered considering he usually tuned such talk out when the family got together for the holidays. Of course, his brother and father found the whole thing utterly fascinating, but he usually had the same expression on his face as Veronica displayed right now. Eyes glazed over, and a glued-on plastic smile.

When the waiter brought the check, Richard almost cried out with relief. A chuckle escaped his lips when Veronica sighed. He'd managed to bore her right out of wanting to ask for a second date. The way she refused to make eye contact only confirmed his opinion.

"It looks like I monopolized all of tonight's conversation. Maybe next time, you can tell me more about yourself. How does that sound? Maybe tomorrow?" Richard leaned forward, eyes round and hopeful. He made his best impression of a love-struck teenager, laying it on thick enough even for gold-digging Veronica to be turned off.

"I'm sorry, Richard. I've already got plans for tomorrow. How about I message you later?"

"Oh," Richard looked down, trying to contain his glee. "Alright. I had a nice time tonight. How about you?"

"The best." She tipped her wrist as if to check the time, but she wasn't even wearing a watch. "Look, Richard, I'm sorry to cut this short, but I really have to get going."

"Sure." Richard leaped from his seat, dropped three hundred dollar bills inside the check folder, and rounded the table to help Veronica with her chair. "I'll walk you down."

"That's okay; I need to visit the ladies' room first. Good night, Richard." Veronica leaned over to give him an air kiss before turning on her high heel and walking away, hips swaying seductively, her head turning from side to side, probably searching for her next victim.

Richard retreated to a dark corner of the bar where he had a clear view of the dance floor. The bartender brought him the seltzer he ordered, and he sat back to watch over Anne-Marie's date. He should have left when Veronica did, but he couldn't make himself go just yet.

Maybe he was feeling a bit masochistic, pining for a woman who could never be his. Perhaps he wanted to feel jealousy rather than the crushing, lonely emptiness that suddenly enveloped him. Like a spoiled child having a tantrum for attention, any feeling was better than no feelings at all.

Anne-Marie's innocence stirred something inside him that he thought didn't exist. She didn't fawn over him or look at him differently when she found out he had money—quite the opposite. She seemed to push him farther away, putting barrier after barrier between them. Maybe that was why she'd accepted a date with George.

Figures that he'd come to this conclusion too late. If he'd known, then he never would have asked her to work for him. But then, he probably wouldn't have realized just how special she was. Not that he knew her all that well; he just had a gut feeling. The kind of feeling he usually only got when a business opportunity appeared too good to be true but worked out in his favor anyway.

He tipped the bottle of seltzer against his lips, letting the bubbly liquid trickle across his tongue. Maybe Anne-Marie had been right when she'd asked him if he were some creepy guy when they first met. Staring at her from the shadows certainly made him feel like he fell into that category. Yet, he couldn't force himself to move away from the agony of hope lost.

Watching George's hands caress her on the dancefloor set his body on fire. He wanted to punch George for being so familiar with her while he wished he could trade places with him and do the same. Richard groaned in agony and closed his eyes as their mouths moved toward each other.

Richard turned, unable to torture himself any longer. As soon as he finished his drink, he'd discreetly leave.

Anne-Marie had made her choice, and it wasn't him. He'd just have to learn to deal with it.

CHAPTER 8
ANNE-MARIE

The music was hard to hear over the hammering of Anne-Marie's heart. Never before had she felt a man's strength and power envelop her body and make her feel helpless. Yet George effortlessly overtook all of her senses. No longer did she even remember the soreness of her ankle as George held her so tightly, her feet barely touched the polished floor.

His hand moved up her back, leaving a trail of warmth in its place. Her skin tingled, and her hands unconsciously tightened around his neck. This was what she'd hoped to share with Daniel, the reason she'd flown halfway across the country to be with him. She felt special, appreciated, maybe even loved, something she hadn't felt since her father died.

George leaned in closer and breathed deeply. His voice, low and husky, sounded right next to her ear, tickling her. "You smell amazing." His hand came up over her shoulder, leaving the fabric to touch the bare skin of her neck. Almost a whisper across her skin, he cupped her jaw and tilted her head toward his.

Leaning forward, his piercing gaze never left hers until he came close. Lashes, every girl would envy, fluttered until his eyes almost closed, leaving just a sparkle of his iris remaining. His breath caressed her lips, almost inviting her to pull away if she wanted to stop.

Anne-Marie's mind completely blanked, inhaling the scent of the red wine he'd consumed with dinner, intoxicating and inviting at the same time. Maybe this was God's plan for her all along, the reason she'd wanted to fly to Texas. Daniel had merely been the carrot, whereas George could be the real destination.

Anne-Marie didn't even realize she'd closed the scant space between them. The feel of his soft lips barely touching hers caused a small groan of pleasure to escape before it even registered in her mind.

George seemed pleased by her response. He threaded his fingers in her hair, pulling her even closer to him. His lips parted, his tongue delved deep inside her mouth.

Unexpectedly, Anne-Marie's nerves came alive, as if electricity jolted every nerve ending at his intense touch. She matched his eagerness with her own, enjoying the attention. But it ended nearly as abruptly as it began.

"What's wrong?" she asked, her eyebrows lowering and her head cocking to the side. Her mind felt drunk with her raging hormones.

George's muscles tensed under her hands where they rested against his chest. His voice sounded deeper, huskier than it had before. His hands moved to grab both of her wrists, the tips of his fingers digging into the tender flesh. "We can't stay here. I'm going to rent a room where we can take our time. I want to see the sunrise shine over your body when we wake. I want all of you. Now."

"What? I thought you said you were only in town until this evening." Anne-Marie's languid thoughts only latched on to part of what George proposed. The intensity of his stare startled her. His eyes flicked toward the restaurant's entrance, appearing as though he were gauging how fast he could haul her out of there.

"I'll change my plans. I want to spend the night with you, Anne-Marie. I haven't felt this way in a long time, and I'm not stupid enough to walk away now."

Finally comprehending George's indecent proposal, Anne-Marie stiffened and ineffectually tried to pull away.

His grip tightened painfully, making the tips of her fingers begin to tingle. "No, George. I think you've mistaken me altogether."

"How could I possibly misinterpret that kiss. You want me as badly as I want you. We're both adults; there's nothing wrong with us enjoying each other's company." Spittle sprayed from his lips, peppering Anne-Marie's face. He pulled her wrists against his chest, daring her to refuse him.

Understanding his intention, albeit belatedly, Anne-Marie relaxed. Plastering on a coy smile, even though every fiber of her being wanted to scream out in terror, she played to his ego. As soon as she felt his grip slacken, she jerked her arms out of his reach and took a step back. "I think you've come to the wrong conclusion, George. I have no intention of sleeping with you. I thought this was a simple dinner date. You're the one who has changed the rules. Not me."

George's features darkened with anger. His menacing voice lowered as he leaned in, so only she could hear his next words. "What kind of tease are you? That kiss was not reserved just for friends. You want me. Are you going to deny that?"

"Look, George. I like you; don't get me wrong. I'm just not that kind of girl." Trying her best to console him, she even reached out a hand to touch his bicep. But he brushed her away like a dirty piece of lint. She flinched and wrapped her arms around her middle.

"I don't know what kind of game you're playing at, but I won't stand for it. You can be sure I'll tell Richard what kind of woman he hired. You're nothing but a hussy. I hope you enjoyed your little game. Good night, Anne-Marie." George left her standing alone on the dance floor. She watched his stiff posture move around the tables between herself and the front door.

Anger flared inside her. How could George say that she'd led him on? If anything, she'd been more off-putting than she ever had with anyone else before. Standing alone and exposed as a fool on the dance floor, she made her way back to their table. Just as she reached for her purse, the waiter came up beside her.

"Here's your check, ma'am." He left it on the table and walked away.

Great! I can't believe George left me stuck with the tab. What a class A jerk!

Then it dawned on her that she didn't have any money. Everything Richard had given her for a bonus was either hanging in her closet or stuffed inside the couch cushion.

How was she going to get out of here without getting arrested or doing the dishes?

She sank into her seat, feeling more helpless than ever. Should she call Beatrice and ask her to bail her out? No way. She'd rather die than never hear the end of this from her only friend. Then she remembered the little black card Richard had left on her desk.

Hope sprang up inside her.

Please be in my purse. Please be in my purse.

Her fingers trembled as she unzipped the bag and felt around for the side pocket where she would have placed it for safekeeping. Her fingers touched the blunt edge, and she triumphantly pulled it out.

The solution to her problem rested in her fingers, but did she dare use it? If she did, then she'd have to tell Richard what happened. Could she possibly endure his displeasure again? What choice did she have?

The waiter returned at that moment and plucked the card from her upraised hand. "I'll be right back with your receipt."

"Oh, I..." Anne-Marie let her response die unvoiced; he was already too far away to hear. Besides, she didn't have another option. Thoughts of her couch beckoned. She needed to curl up around a tub of ice cream, watch a sappy movie, and probably cry for the rest of the night. She felt stupid—the worst kind of fool.

How could she have thought this night would end any differently? She should have paid more attention to the warning bells she'd heard back at the office the first time he touched her. But his flattery had punched down her shields. She'd willingly, eagerly even, let her feelings overcome her common sense.

Maybe her mother was right in telling her it was a devil's errand to come to Texas. Perhaps she should go back home to Oregon and try to forget all about the sultry southern heat and the sexy men who wanted to take advantage of her.

The waiter brought back the slip for her to sign. She didn't even look at the total, knowing it would be astronomical. When she got to her apartment, she'd look, but not here, not with a room full of witnesses to her most mortifying night ever. She shoved her copy of the receipt into her purse and stood to leave.

But she paused with indecision. What if George was still outside, lying in wait for her to leave? She couldn't chance it, not in her current state of mind. Already standing, she shifted her direction to head to the bar.

Anne-Marie had to lean between two patrons to catch the bartender's attention. "Could you possibly make me an espresso?"

The bartender didn't even pause with the drink he expertly poured for another customer. He actually winked at her. "Sure thing, ma'am."

After leaving her last ten-dollar bill on the counter, she stepped back and looked around for a place to kill time. The darkest corner of the bar appeared nearly empty, so she made her way over. She sat next to a man who had his back turned and crossed her legs.

Once again, she tugged at the hem of her skirt. When she got home, she planned on burning this outfit. Never again could she wear it and not think about George's touch all over her.

"Ma'am? You forgot your credit card," the waiter from the dining area declared, holding out the card for her.

"Oh, thank you so much. I can't believe I forgot it." Anne-Marie felt heat flare into her cheeks as she discreetly tucked the black card back into her purse.

"Why didn't George pay?" A man's voice asked next to her.

Almost leaping out of her chair, Anne-Marie's mouth spat out the first thing that came to mind. "Richard! What are you doing hiding in the shadows?"

Richard turned until he fully faced her, but he didn't answer her question.

"George had to leave in a hurry. I guess he forgot to pay."

Richard's expression shifted into one Anne-Marie had never seen before. Confusion, pity, anger—maybe all three. "He left? Why? The two of you were having such a good time on the dance floor."

Anne-Marie's eyes widened. She'd have to tell Richard what happened sooner than she planned. "You saw that? What else did you see?"

Richard leaned back in his chair, his arms crossing over his chest. "I saw the two of you kissing. You looked pretty content. What could possibly have come up that was so urgent as to leave without paying?"

Closing her eyes and sighing long and loud through her nose, Anne-Marie waited another second before inhaling. She couldn't look at him, so she left her eyes shut. "Mr. Hansen had other ideas for how we should end the evening. Needless to say, I turned him down, and he didn't like it. He called me a hussy and left. There. Are you happy now? Don't worry about the charges on your card. I'll pay for it out of my next paycheck."

"What happened to the bonus I gave you? Don't tell me you spent it all already."

Anne-Marie's eyes flared open, not liking his tone in the slightest. "No, I didn't spend it all. It happens to be tucked away for safe-keeping in my couch cushion. I would have brought some with me, but I didn't plan on going out to dinner tonight. And I certainly didn't expect to have to pay for said dinner."

Richard's eyes glazed over. His fingers drummed across the tabletop. Finally, he shook his head and exhaled. "I can't work with someone like that. I'll call him tomorrow to cancel our deal. You won't ever have to see him again. And don't worry about the credit card; it's not your problem."

Relief warred with pride. She couldn't let her boss bail her out of her self-imposed situation. He deserved better. Maybe he'd even reconsider keeping her on as his executive assistant. "Rich, you don't have to do that. I'm the one who agreed to go to dinner with him. You shouldn't have to pay for my mistake."

Shaking his head adamantly, looking for all the world like her two-year-old nephew, Richard said, "I brought George into your life, and I'm going to do my best to keep him out of it from now on. Of course, if that's what you want."

"I don't want to go through another evening like this one ever again. Thank you, Rich. You really are a true gentleman." She had to close her mouth before she made any more gushing statements regarding his virtues. She'd already said too much. Luckily, the bartender arrived with her espresso, just as the silence became uncomfortable. "Thank you."

She grabbed the cup like a lifeline and held it between her cold fingers. The heat prickled against her skin, but she didn't set it down. The pain helped her keep focused on the here and now. "Hey. Where's your date? Is she in the bathroom?"

Richard just finished tipping his seltzer water into his mouth. His coughing and sputtering drew the attention of several nearby customers. Anne-Marie held out a napkin for him as water spurted out of his closed lips. His face turned red as he tried to control his breathing until he could swallow the water.

Anne-Marie merely looked at her boss with concern and confusion. Had it only been a coincidence that he choked at the same time as she'd asked her question? Or was there more to his story?

CHAPTER 9

RICHARD

If only Richard would have waited another second before taking a drink, then maybe he might not have made such a commotion. Still, he hadn't known that Anne-Marie had even seen him enter the restaurant, let alone with a date. So much for trying to remain unseen. He'd bungled that up. Big-time.

"I'm sorry, Rich. Are you okay? Do you want me to get you non-carbonated water to soothe your throat?" Anne-Marie sat perched on the edge of her seat. Her concern for his health kept her from realizing how far her skirt had hitched up her thighs.

Trying to be a gentleman, Richard averted his gaze from her lap. This wasn't the time to be perverted or even distracted. Coughing several more times, Richard used the napkin to wipe the tears from the corners of his eyes before dabbing it across his mouth and jaw.

He shook his head and held out his hand to prevent Anne-Marie from moving. "I'm fine." Another bout of coughs threatened to undermine his statement. "I just swallowed wrong."

Finally, regaining his composure, Richard decided to come clean. After all, he didn't want Anne-Marie to feel so bad about her evening. He could distract her by telling his own sordid story.

"My date left me, claiming she had to go to the ladies' room. You couldn't have known that was her excuse, but it just struck me funny when you asked."

"That beautiful woman walked out on you? What an idiot! How long have you known her?" Anne-Marie sat back and shook her head in wonder.

"That's the worst part, Anne-Marie. I didn't know her at all before we met for dinner. I arranged this dinner from a dating app." Richard couldn't look Anne-Marie in the eyes. He felt so stupid.

"Did you come here to spy on me or something?"

"What? No! I didn't have any idea George would bring you here. I just wanted to have a nice evening with someone who didn't expect anything from me—someone who I could have a pleasant evening with."

"And did you?"

"Did I—what?"

"Have a nice evening?"

This time Richard laughed with real feeling. Should he tell her what he'd done? She'd probably think he was a bigger fool, but he'd only have to agree. "Not in the slightest. I told Veronica I was an accountant. Then I spent the entire evening telling stories my father and brother shared over Thanksgiving dinner about their clients' tax returns."

Anne-Marie's mouth hung open with disbelief. Her face transformed into radiant beauty as she threw her head back and laughed. "No wonder she dumped you! Are you crazy? Why didn't you just try to be yourself? You're a lot of fun to be around."

"I'm glad you think so, but she was just a gold digger. She didn't care about me at all. I tried to make myself so boring she'd do anything to keep me from asking for a second date."

Another chuckle escaped from Anne-Marie's lips. "We're quite the pair. Aren't we? I don't know how I can be so wrong with my guy picker. It must be broken. I really am a donkey!"

"Huh? Have you been drinking?"

Rolling her eyes, she leaned forward to put her cup on the table before she rested her elbows on her knees. In almost a whisper, she said, "No, I haven't had a drop of liquor.

"Look, I came to Texas because a cowboy told me he loved me. It turns out he loves every girl he meets. Then tonight," she gestured widely with one arm to encompass the entirety of the restaurant, "I thought God used Daniel like a carrot in front of a donkey to lure me into coming to Texas so that I could meet George. Only, he turned out to be a more prosperous version of Daniel, but just as low-down, dirty, rotten when it comes to women." She dropped her arm dejectedly and added, "I must be broken. That's it. I'm broken."

Richard reached out to touch her knee. "No, Anne-Marie, don't say stuff like that. I think you're amazing. You're funny. You're beautiful. You're kind."

Anne-Marie stared at his hand for a few seconds before her eyes lifted to meet his earnest gaze. "Do you realize you just described the best attributes of a dog? That's hardly comforting, Rich."

"Don't they say dogs are man's best friend? You can hardly go wrong then. Don't you think?"

Anne-Marie shook her head slowly, a chuckle escaping from her lips. "You say the dumbest things, Rich. But you mean well, and I like you a lot. Does that mean you want me to be your best friend?"

Latching on to her olive branch, Richard held on for dear life. "You'd be my only friend in Houston."

"I find that really hard to believe. I'm sure you've got people lining up to be your BFF."

"Right. More like they're lining up for my ATM. Don't you realize how few people I can really trust? Once anyone finds out I have money, that's all they see anymore. But you're not like that."

Anne-Marie's eyes dropped along with her shoulders. She shifted her legs until Richard's hand fell away. "Then why do you want me to be your friend?"

"What's that supposed to mean?" Richard didn't understand her sudden change of mood. What was she hiding from him? Did he honestly want to know?

Exhaling loudly, Anne-Marie kept her gaze locked on her clasped fingers. "Think about the two days I've known you, Rich. Yesterday, I asked for a sign-on bonus—granted, that was Beatrice's idea, but I was the one who asked. Then today,

I used your credit card to pay for an extravagant dinner. It sure looks like I'm only hanging around for the money."

"Hardly! You've fought me every step of the way. Do you forget that I practically had to chase you down to give you the check yesterday?"

He spotted a twitch lifting the corner of her mouth. He knew he'd looked like a fool chasing after her, but he'd do it again if it made her smile. "If I hadn't come outside, then you would've told Beatrice to drive away without it. Don't bother denying it, either. I saw the look on your face. Plus, you tried to give it back, remember?

"Gold-diggers don't do that. They take the money and run. You took the money, but then you showed up for work today. We hadn't even signed employment paperwork—I wouldn't have had a legal leg to stand on. But you did. You came to work because you're honest. I'll not hear about you maligning yourself. Ever. Do I make myself clear?"

Barely above a whisper, "Yes."

Daring, Richard lifted his hand to cup her chin; he raised her face until she looked at him. "I know I can trust you. Can you trust me?"

"Yes." Her eyes drifted away from his face.

"What's wrong, Anne-Marie? Friends don't keep secrets from one another. You have to spill it."

"Maybe I don't want to be friends. Maybe I want more. But I can't because you're my boss, and you made it quite clear yesterday that you're not interested in me." Her eyes hardened like sharpened steel. "There, is that honest enough for you?"

Richard flinched at her reprimand. But her words struck him deep in the heart. She wanted to be more than friends, and she somehow got the impression that he didn't want her. "You're right. Maybe I don't want us to be friends."

He dropped out of his chair onto his knees in front of her. Being uncommonly bold, he took her face between both of his hands and pulled her toward him. He wasn't going to leave anything to chance this time.

His lips crushed against hers, his tongue flicking across her lips and tasting her espresso. But he didn't want to press his luck, especially since she didn't make any move to kiss him back. He softened his hold, barely touching her face or lips at all. With a final peck, he rocked back onto his heels. "Can you honestly say I'm not interested in you now?"

Tears crested over Anne-Marie's lower lashes and dropped onto her thighs, staining her sheer pantyhose. Richard wanted to comfort her, but he feared he'd only make things worse. Another tear fell, but he caught it on his palm. "Don't cry, Anne-Marie. Please don't tell me that I've ruined any chance I've had to be with you."

"You don't even know me, Rich. You're just placating me now, and that's not helping."

"Placa—," Richard abruptly stood and held out his hand. "Come on." Wiggling his fingers impatiently, he almost cried out with relief when Anne-Marie's palm crossed over his. Curling his fingers around her small hand, he pulled her from the chair with one hand while he used the other to grab her purse and hold it out to her.

"What are you doing?"

"We're getting out of here. We need to talk, and I'm tired of having an audience." Richard led her out of the restaurant and out to the elevator.

"Where are we going?"

"My house." Richard punched the elevator button and cursed under his breath for how long the lift took to get to the penthouse.

"Oh, no, no, no. George already propositioned me tonight; I'm not going through this again. I'm going home. We can talk at the office tomorrow."

Anne-Marie tried to slip her hand out of his. She tugged harder when Richard's grip tightened. The elevator doors opened, and he hauled her inside the empty space.

"Didn't you hear me, Richard? I'm not going home with you. I'm tired, and I want to go to bed." Her cheeks flushed bright pink. "Alone!"

Richard's laughter echoed inside the confined space. "I'm not taking you home to ravish you, silly. When I say I want to talk, you can trust that's all we're going to do. We need to set some things straight, and I don't want any interruptions. Namely, Jimmy walking in on our little heart-to-heart. Will you come home with me? Please?" Richard tried coercing her, then cajoling her, now he wasn't above begging. Not if it meant she'd give him a chance.

The elevator doors opened into the lobby. Richard let Anne-Marie step out ahead of him and almost ran into her back as she came to an abrupt stop. Looking over her head, he spotted the problem. Stepping around Anne-Marie, Richard placed himself between her and George.

"You have some nerve loitering here in the lobby for Anne-Marie," Richard started, he didn't raise his voice, but his aggressive stance didn't leave his intent unnoticed.

George stepped forward, his face turning purple and his eyes almost bugging out of his head. "You're defending that hussy? You don't know what you're dealing with. She totally led me on so that she could get a free meal out of me. All I wanted was a little compensation, but she practically slapped me in the face for suggesting it. Even after she threw herself at me."

"You don't need to tell me what happened, George. Even if your descriptions are a bit off, I saw the whole thing. I was there to witness it all." Richard paused to let that sink in before delivering his parting line. "I was going to wait until tomorrow, but seeing as you're so eager to hang around, I might as well tell you now."

"What's that? Are you going to tell me that you and that hussy have some sick hustle? Do you get your jollies out of dangling her in front of your prospective clients? That's sick, man. Just sick."

"I think you're confusing me with yourself. Anne-Marie and I are friends first, as well as co-workers. Nothing has ever gone on between us. But you, you are the real piece of work. You come to my business, pick up on my assistant, and then have the nerve to tell me that I'm playing a sick game.

"What would have happened if I hadn't been at the restaurant tonight? What would you have said or done with Anne-Marie when she came out of the elevator expecting to go home in peace? Would you have forced her into your car and taken her to that hotel room you propositioned her with? Is that the kind of man you are?

"I don't really want to hear your answer. But my answer to you is this. We're through. I refuse to do business with men like you. I only work with honest, caring people, not scumbags like you."

George's complexion managed to change to a deeper red at each of Richard's statements. "You're going to regret crossing me, Richard. That...that...hussy is not going to be worth the trouble you just brought on yourself for maligning my character in such a manner. You'll see. You'll pay for your insults. I'll see to it."

George turned on his heel before punching the door frame to get it to open. A fraction of an inch to the right, and he would have put his fist through the glass opening itself.

Richard spared a glance behind him to see Anne-Marie's ashen face. "Please tell me you're coming home with me."

CHAPTER 10
ANNE-MARIE

Anne-Marie didn't know if she should clap for Richard's spectacular performance or cry in fear at George's threats. What she did know for sure was that she did not want to be alone tonight. Not if George was still in town and full of fury at Richard defending her honor.

Nodding, she didn't have the voice to say anything out loud. She clung to Richard's arm, almost in the same manner as she'd seen Veronica do inside the restaurant. She hated feeling weak, but she appreciated Richard's strength. Never before had a man stood up for her as he had just done. It made her feel grateful and sorry at the same time.

If only she just would have refused George's offer for dinner, then none of this would have happened. What if she'd just cost Richard a lucrative deal? Could she live with herself for creating such a liability for her new boss? Would he regret his decision come morning?

She followed Richard to the valet station and shivered against him as they waited for the car to be brought around. The valet held the passenger door open for her, and she gratefully sank into the plush leather seat. The solid thump of the door closing gave her a measure of security. But Richard sliding behind the steering wheel made her feel even better.

"Oh! What about Wilson? He's probably still waiting for me to leave. I should call him and let him know he can go home." She searched in her purse for the card Wilson had given her with his number.

"Don't worry. I've got his number on speed dial." Richard tapped a couple of buttons, and Wilson's voice filled the car speakers after he answered the call. "Wilson, Rich here. I'll be taking Anne-Marie home tonight. Have a nice evening with Leslie and the kids."

Of course, Richard would know all about his employees' personal lives. Just another example of how much he cared for the people around him. As if she needed more proof that Richard was the upstanding guy everyone told her about.

She fumbled with her seatbelt, making several attempts before the latch clicked in place. Tremors rushed through her body, forcing her to tuck her hands close to her body to keep them from shaking. Her purse, forgotten, fell from her lap onto the floor. Was this what it felt like to be in shock?

"Are you cold?" Richard asked, his hand already moving to adjust the temperature.

"Only a little." Another bout of tremors shook her frame. She clenched her teeth together to prevent them from clacking together and giving sound to her fib. Why was she overreacting like this?

Maybe because she'd never had someone she'd just met turn into a monster right before her eyes. True, Daniel had lied and cheated on her, but he never got aggressive with her, nor did he threaten her. She turned her face to watch the street lights pass by. It didn't matter where they drove, just as long as they got as far away from George and the memory of his fury.

Even when she closed her eyes, she could see the rage shining brightly, directed at her, and then at Richard. She'd brought this trouble to Richard's doorstep, but she didn't know how to fix it. "I was thinking—." Her bottom lip tipped up between her teeth. Should she say it out loud? Maybe Richard hadn't heard her.

"What's on your mind, Anne-Marie?"

Although he meant his hand to be comforting on her shoulder, she hadn't expected it. She flinched, and the warmth of his hand went away. "Hey, are you okay? Talk to me, Anne-Marie."

"I should go back to Oregon. I don't think I'm doing any good here in Texas. In fact, I've only caused trouble for the people trying to help me." Anne-Marie's words convinced her even as she spoke them. They felt right, better than this empty, fearfulness inside her.

At least in Oregon, she had her old friends. Granted, they had mostly moved on; they had families of their own. She was the only one left single of her core friends. Which was probably the reason she'd gone chasing after Daniel. The idea of a runaway romance sounded so alluring. Too bad the whole thing only left a sour taste in her mouth.

"You're doing me good," quietly, almost to himself, Richard replied. He never looked toward Anne-Marie. His eyes remained glued to the road ahead of them. But his hands gave him away—they clutched the steering wheel tightly. The tendons popped out along the backs of his hands to be lost underneath the fancy cuffs of his expensive suit.

"You can't possibly mean that. I just cost you a lucrative partnership. You said yourself that it was going to make a killing." Anne-Marie gulped in air, trying valiantly to keep from crying. She wasn't a baby; tears wouldn't help.

"I don't want to talk about this right now. When we get to my place, we can delve into it further. Tell me about Oregon." Richard darted a glance over to her, a smile playing across his full lips. The passing streetlights showed the bristles of hair growing along his jawline. Anne-Marie wanted to reach out and touch it, but she kept her hands tucked along her sides.

"I lived there all my life. It's the best of everything. We have the mountains for snowboarding, the high desert, the Willamette Valley where some of the finest wines are grown, the rainforest, and the rocky coastline. Out of all of the places I've seen pictures of, I just kept saying that it all looked like Oregon."

A small, pleased sound came from Richard's throat. His hands relaxed on the wheel. "Sounds interesting. I haven't been there myself. Maybe we could make a trip back there, and you can show me around."

"I have a brother and sister and my mom, who still live there. My brother moved up to Portland and opened his own microbrewery. My sister moved to Bend to be near her husband's family. My mom is retired and spends all of her time gardening."

"And that leaves you. What did you plan to do in Oregon? Before you went chasing after your dream, that is."

"Ugh! Don't remind me about Daniel. I can't believe I was so gullible to believe him. My mom warned me, but I didn't listen." Anne-Marie sighed, clamping her mouth shut by trapping her bottom lip between her teeth. She didn't need to keep rehashing her sordid history with her boss. Surely, he didn't want to hear about it.

The car rolled to a stop at the traffic light. The engine purred like a kitten. Richard turned to face Anne-Marie, his expression more serious than she'd ever seen it before. "I'm glad you came to Texas. I think God has had a hand in this whole crazy adventure. Who are we to try to pick apart His reasoning? We should just see where His plan leads us and enjoy the journey."

Anne-Marie's eyes widened, and her mouth dropped open slightly. "Do you really think God had this planned? Or are you just saying that because of what I said earlier?"

"You might have to remind me of your earlier comment, but I thought that the moment I saw you being walked by that pack of dogs. Besides, you said yourself that Reba's behavior was completely out of character. What if a little guardian angel pushed her to jump on me so we could meet? I mean, strange things have been happening since the moment you crossed my path."

"I'm not sure if I can survive anything stranger than what's already gone on. Pretty soon, you'll be begging me to pack my bags and leave so you can have your simple life back."

Laughter erupted from Richard, long enough that Anne-Marie's lips pulled back against her better judgment. She hadn't tried to be funny, but it obviously struck a chord in Richard. Either that or he was just crazy—her kind of crazy, apparently.

They made several turns before they came to a gated driveway. Richard waited a few seconds for the gate to open before pulling into the circular driveway. "This is it. Home, sweet home."

Anne-Marie ogled out the window, her face almost pressed against the glass to look up and up the columned front of the massive wrap-around porch. "This looks like it could be a movie set for Gone With the Wind. Was that your inspiration?"

"Never seen it before." Richard unbuckled and let himself out of the car.

Of course not, that's a chick-flick.

Anne-Marie watched him walk around the hood and open the passenger door. Belatedly, she rushed to get her buckle undone, but it refused to cooperate. "Sorry. I seem to be stuck."

Richard leaned over her, his face directly in front of her. Heat radiated from him as if the sun lived inside his skin. Anne-Marie sucked in a startled breath, inhaling his cologne and infusing her lungs with his unique, masculine scent. Her heart hammered, probably loud enough for him to hear since he was so close. The strap released, and Richard's hand trailed across her arm along with it.

"I should get that looked at. Can't have you getting stuck in the car. Are you ready to go inside?" He held out his hand for her, so gallant in his offering.

Anne-Marie's eyebrow quirked, but she took his hand. "I bet you say that to all of the ladies you bring here." The moment the words slipped out, she wanted to take them back.

Richard's fingers tightened involuntarily against hers. "You're only the second one. The first one didn't end well, obviously. Maybe we can get this right."

That wasn't the answer she expected. Again, her mouth refused to listen to her brain. "Only the second? Did you just move here?"

Richard laughed, his fingers gripping hers more naturally as he relaxed. "No. I've lived here for nine years. I had it built with the help of a designer. I'll have to ask if she was a fan of that movie, though. I just thought it looked regal, manly even."

"More like elegant and timeless."

"You're still shivering, even though it's at least seventy-five outside. How does a hot chocolate in front of the fireplace sound?" Richard slung his arm across her shoulders, letting his wrist hang slack by her jaw, not threatening in the least.

Anne-Marie wanted to snuggle into his side, like a kitten seeking comfort in a storm. "Sounds like a dream. I haven't had hot cocoa since I was little. Mom met us outside with hot chocolate when we walked home from school in the snow. Best memory ever."

"Maybe we can make another best memory, then." Richard led the way up the grand stairs leading to the double-door entry. He opened one oversized black door and let it swing inward. "After you."

Anne-Marie stepped inside to have an unobstructed view of the foyer. "Definitely inspired by the movie. We're going to have to watch it, so you'll know what I'm talking about."

Richard stepped in behind her and shut the door. "Already planning movies together, huh? Don't you think you might be moving a bit too fast? I might get the wrong impression about you."

Anne-Marie twirled around, her face stricken with guilt. "I'm sorry, Rich. I didn't mean to imply—"

"Relax, Anne-Marie. I was only teasing." He grabbed her hand and pulled her down the hall. "This is my favorite room in the house."

The light flicked on as soon as they crossed the threshold. Books lined two walls, and a fireplace took up half of another one with an oversized mantle covered with trinkets. Walking across the room, Anne-Marie picked up a small gold-framed picture of an elegant young woman. Turning around, she asked, "Is this someone from your family?"

Richard took the picture from her hands. His thumb caressed the frame lovingly. His voice came out soft with a loving memory. "My gran when she was younger than me. I think she was seventeen here. This was the day she got married to her first husband. He died right after this from the Spanish Flu."

"That's terrible. Do you have a picture of him?"

"No. A year later, she met and married my grandpapa. She loved John, but she was in love with Kenneth. She'd loved him all her life, but he didn't come forward to tell her he felt the same until after she married John." Richard put the frame back on the mantle and turned to face Anne-Marie. "She always said God works in mysterious ways. My gran was never wrong."

"You can't deny that grandmas have special wisdom about life. They've seen so many hardships and lived through some tough times. We have it so good in comparison."

"You got that right." Leading her to the couch, he said, "Get comfy, and I'll start the fire."

CHAPTER 11
RICHARD

Richard never imagined this evening would end with Anne-Marie curled up on the couch next to him. Heck, he never even thought she'd know where he lived. Time and again, his eyes glanced up to Gran's picture, where she appeared to be smiling warmly down at them.

Could this be what she had in mind for him when she told him to build a grand house? He never wanted to get married; his plans didn't include a wife or family. But this house could undoubtedly hold an army of children should he ever change his mind.

If he ever wanted to prove himself to his father, then he had to do it alone. No distractions. No relationships other than with business partners. Lillith had proven to be his biggest mistake—one he didn't plan to repeat.

Yet, Anne-Marie...she was different. He cast a sidelong glance at her where she held her cocoa mug close to her chest, and her eyes stared unblinking at the fire. What was going on inside her mind? He never could tell. She didn't act or think like any of the women who had come into his life.

She was reserved, too reserved for her own good. He wanted to show her what life had to offer. It seemed as though she'd only tasted bitterness, not the sweetness of happiness. What was he thinking? He didn't have any experience with happiness other than the joy he got in giving money away. How could he possibly teach her anything?

Her toes peeked out from beneath the blanket draped across her lap. The fire put out plenty of heat, but the rise of her skirt bothered her. He'd given her the quilt out of courtesy, not because he hadn't enjoyed the view. Still, the grateful look she'd cast at him made him feel like a superhero. Such a simple gesture, but she'd acted as though he'd offered her the world.

He'd never spent an evening in silence with a woman. Yet, she appeared perfectly content. Even more relaxed than he'd ever seen her before. He liked it, but he wanted more.

Richard almost regretted speaking when Anne-Marie jumped at his first word. "When we were in the car, you asked why I'd so willingly throw away my partnership with George."

Anne-Marie's toes retreated under the blanket as she shifted to face Richard. "Yes. I feel terrible about the whole sordid mess."

"Don't." He held up his hand to stop her from arguing. He could see the apologies already wanting to come out of her mouth. Turning toward the fire, he weighed his words carefully.

"I think you just saved me a lot of unwanted scandals. If George tried to do that to you tonight, how many other women has he taken advantage of elsewhere? If our companies were tied together, then I'd be under the same umbrella of scrutiny. That's not the image I want to have. I've worked entirely too hard to keep my public life as professional as possible." Richard continued to stare into the fire as if it could show him the future he narrowly avoided.

With a voice so soft, Richard could have pretended not to hear; Anne-Marie asked, "What about your private life? Is that kept professional as well?"

Breath whooshed out of Richard. Bitterness filled his mouth at the question. "What private life? Other than the painful interlude with Lillith, my whole life is my work."

The sound of the wind howling outside broke the silence surrounding them. Softly, almost under her breath, Anne-Marie said, "Lillith. The devil's consort. Interesting."

"What's that?" Once again, Richard wondered where Anne-Marie was going with her random comment.

She shook her head; a whisp of a chuckle escaped her lips. Sitting up straighter, she turned to face Richard fully. "All of this talk about God and fate got me thinking. My mom told me I was on the devil's errand to chase after Daniel. Then you tell me that your last girlfriend's name was Lillith. Is it too much of a coincidence that the stories all say the devil's consort was named Lillith? But that would mean—" Anne-Marie turned away, her cheeks flushing a bright red as she held her hand over her mouth.

Richard believed he could follow where Anne-Marie's story was going. He needed her to say it out loud. "Finish that thought."

"Nothing, it's just silliness. Stupid, really." She cut her hand across the space between them, ending with it dropping to her lap. Her eyes narrowed as she squared her shoulders and asked, "Why are you running from your private life? Do you enjoy spending every waking moment making money?"

Richard's nostrils flared as he sucked in a quick breath. He could get whiplash with how fast she changed the subject. "I'm not running from anything. I've got an empire to build. That takes careful attention. It's a full-time job and then some."

Defiantly shaking her head, Anne-Marie wasn't going to let this go. "An empire? Don't you already have millions of dollars? What are you trying to prove?"

"Billions."

"What?" Anne-Marie put her empty mug down. Her fingers gripped the edge of the blanket in a stranglehold, probably wishing it were his neck.

"You said I had millions of dollars. That's not true. I have billions." Richard managed to answer with a straight face, even though he could tell she was getting annoyed with his deflection from answering her real question.

She threw her hands up in the air and rolled her eyes. "You see? Billions! Oh, brother. You're totally proving my point. I'll ask again: what are you trying to prove? Who are you trying to impress?"

Right at this moment, Anne-Marie reminded him of a Pitt bull. She went straight for the jugular and latched on. No amount of pushing or resisting would make her unlock from this line of questioning. Did he really want to let her in on his deepest, darkest secret?

Would she tell him that he had been stupid to waste so much of his life? Probably. Did he deserve it? Probably. Did he agree with her? Definitely.

"Fine. You want to know the truth? It's my father. My wildly successful CPA father." The bitterness was back stronger than ever. Even saying it out loud made his pulse pound in his neck. He could hear the wild thudding of his heart in his eardrums.

Anne-Marie reached over and rested her palm against the bare flesh of his forearm. She scooted closer to him, almost leaning against his side. "Why, Richard? If he's so successful, then he'd be happy that you've done the same for yourself. How could that be wrong?"

Richard jumped up from the couch, startling Anne-Marie back to her side. He paced several times before he answered, "Because I didn't join his company. That was the plan—his plan for me. I'm the oldest. Of course, I'd follow in my father's footsteps and take over the business one day. He had it all worked out until the day I told him I wasn't interested."

He stopped pacing to face Anne-Marie. Now that he started talking, it was as if the dam's crack widened, and the rushing waters forced the sides away until a torrent overflowed. "You'd think I'd just run a knife through his heart with how he reacted. In fact, I thought he was having a heart attack. All the color left his face, and his mouth opened and closed without any sound coming out.

"Do you know what he finally said to me?"

Anne-Marie shook her head slowly.

"He said I'd be nothing without him. I'd never have anything to call my own. He told me to leave and never come begging for money when my little dreams failed. That's how much confidence he had in me."

"That's awful, Richard. No parent should put that kind of burden on their children. You know he was only speaking from the pain of disappointment, right? He didn't mean any of it, Richard. You can't let that one moment taint the rest of your life." Anne-Marie uncurled her legs and set her feet on the ground. Tossing the blanket aside, Richard saw more of her thighs than he had before, but she didn't seem to notice. She stood and put her hands on both of his biceps.

"He meant it. Every word." He saw Anne-Marie shaking her head, which meant he had to tell her the rest. "I know he meant it because he says it every time the family gets together. Even though my brother, Charles, went to work for my father, it wasn't enough. Do you know what he says to everyone?"

He didn't wait for any response; his anger began to make his words spill out faster and faster. "Whenever we go anywhere together, Father claps Charles on the shoulder and introduces him as the best son any father could ask for. A chip off the old block. He shares all of Charles's successes as though they were his own. And Charles just sits there and grins at me, eating it all up."

In a faint whisper, Anne-Marie asked, "How does your father introduce you?"

Scoffing rudely, Richard shook his head. "If he ever does get around to introducing me, he says something like, 'Oh, yeah. This is Richard, but he takes after his mother. Unreliable and scattered. Too willful for his own good. He'll see, he'll see. He majored in Entrepreneurial Business. What kind of a cockamamie degree is that? Now Charles, here, he graduated top of his class from Harvard. Can you beat that? Fine son. Fine son, indeed. Couldn't ask for any better.'"

"That's terrible, Richard. I'm so sorry. I'd love to give your father a piece of my mind. He doesn't deserve to have you as his son. Do you know that? You're way too good for him."

"Do you want to know the worst part?"

"I don't know. How could it get worse?"

Richard laughed without humor. "Charles paid someone to do all of his homework and take all of his tests. He didn't earn the top of his class at Harvard; he bought it. But Father doesn't seem to notice that Charles doesn't even like working at the CPA firm. Once again, Charles pays people to do his job and then takes all of the credit. It's disgusting; that's what it is. And he doesn't try to hide it, but Father doesn't even see it."

Anne-Marie shook her head, almost in slow motion. She was trying to understand his crazy family dynamic, that much Richard could see. "Maybe he's too proud to admit that Charles isn't all that he's talked him up to be. Or maybe, he's praised him so many times that he actually has convinced himself that it's true. What does your mother say about all of this?"

Her question caught him off-guard. His shoulders drooped, and the fight went out of him. Trust Anne-Marie to hit on the one thing that would cause him the most agony. He turned to face the fire, the heat barely registering on his instantly cold flesh. The air barely penetrated his lungs, and his heart clenched painfully. Quietly, almost to himself, he half-turned and answered, "She can't say anything to defend herself or me. She left when I was ten."

From his peripheral vision, he saw her hand immediately stretch out toward him. He'd resumed his pacing, out of her reach. Hurt and understanding etched lines across her forehead when she tipped up her head to console him. "Oh, Richard. I'm so sorry. I know how hard it is to lose a parent, but you were only ten. That had to be about the worst age to lose her."

Nodding, Richard felt the aching wash over him as if he were still that ten-year-old kid. He kept talking, "After she was gone, Father poured more time than ever building his empire. He spent all his time at the office. Eventually, he hired nannies to take care of us, but he refused to let us go to boarding school. Not that Father would have noticed.

"Sometimes, I wonder if our relationship would have been better if he'd shipped us off somewhere. By the time I went to college, his net worth was over a billion dollars, but his emotional wealth was bankrupt. Neither Charles nor I had any kind of father-son relationship with him."

Richard's whole body shuddered as if feeling his mother's ghost pass through him. He hardly ever spoke about her; the pain rushed back whenever he did. Nobody ever wanted to feel as helpless as he had when his father told him that his mother was never coming home. She had been his best friend, his confidant, his inspiration. Then she left him alone without a word of goodbye.

CHAPTER 12
ANNE-MARIE

Anne-Marie clenched her teeth together, hoping to prevent the yawn, which clawed its way up her throat, from coming out. Her eyes watered with the effort, to no avail. Raising the back of her hand to cover her mouth, she shook her head. "I'm so sorry. I swear I'm not bored. The heat from the fire is making me sleepy."

Richard immediately responded with concern. "No, I'm the one who should be sorry. I've selfishly kept you up too late. You probably want to get home so you can relax and go to bed." He looked around in confusion.

The idea of being alone in her apartment made the hair on her arms stand on end. What if George somehow figured out where she lived? He could be lying in wait for her. Who knew what that man was capable of? She certainly didn't want to find out. Unsuccessfully, she tried to suppress a shiver of fear.

"I don't want to go home. Would it be okay if I spent the night?"

That didn't come out right. Was he thinking I was trying to proposition him?

She sat on the couch, patting the cushion, and added, "I could sleep right here. No bother at all. Besides, with the way the wind is howling outside, I don't think it'd be safe for either of us to be on the roads."

"The wind?" Richard turned, his expression almost comical as though he hadn't even noticed the commotion going on outside. "Oh, yeah. The weather reports did say there was a tropical depression heading this way. I guess it finally got here. Anyway, don't be silly. I won't have you sleeping on my couch. We're not in college anymore. I've got six spare bedrooms, for Pete's sake. Let me give you a quick tour."

His mood considerably lightened now that they weren't discussing his dysfunctional family. She thought she had problems; they seemed tame compared to his. More than ever, she realized the general public assumed that wealthy people didn't have problems, but she could see how that money had shattered Richard's family.

She followed him up the stairs, letting her fingers trail along the silky smooth mahogany railing. So much luxury, yet so much empty isolation. It made her wish she could take some of his loneliness away, but she couldn't compete with women like Lillith. She might not have been the right girl for Richard, but at least Lillith had the proper family pedigree to be readily accepted into his wealthy circle.

"I think you'll like this room," Richard said, coming to an abrupt stop several doors away from the top of the stairs. "It has a beautiful view of the gardens out back. You'll see it when you wake up. Can I get you anything?"

If she hadn't been paying attention, she would have walked right into him. Smiling at the thought, she took a second to say, "Do you have anything I could change into for sleeping? I'm sick of this outfit." She didn't ever want to wear it again but thought it would be wise to wear something while sleeping. "A shirt maybe, or sweats. I'm not picky."

His grin matched hers. "I think I can scrounge something up. Just a sec." Pushing himself away from where he leaned against the wall, he took two steps across the hall and opened the door opposite of hers.

Anne-Marie leaned forward to catch a glimpse of his bedroom. She guessed he'd have large, dominating furniture, so she wasn't surprised to find exactly that. What she didn't count on was the window seat with thick cushions and an open book resting on it as if he'd been interrupted. What was he reading? Had she read it, as well?

She hadn't even realized her curiosity had her moving into the room until Richard almost bumped into her when he walked out of his closet. "Oh, I'm sorry for intruding." She pointed toward the book and said, "I wanted to see what you were reading."

He turned to look as if he didn't remember, either. He bent over and plucked the novel from the cushion. Handing it over to her, he said, "You caught me."

Anne-Marie turned the book over to see a magical realism series she hadn't heard of before. Raising her eyebrows, she said, "I didn't take you for a fantasy fiction reader. Huh. What else are you hiding?"

Richard laughed, holding out one of his shirts. "You caught me. I'm an international man of mystery. Will this teeshirt work? I couldn't find a clean pair of sweats."

"Yes. As I said, I'm not picky." Her fingers brushed against his, an unexpected warmth against her cold flesh as she took the offered clothing. "Here's your book back. I wouldn't want you to miss the ending."

His eyes never left hers when he took the book from her. "Some endings are worth waiting for." He turned, tossing the novel onto his nightstand. Still facing away from her, he asked, "What time do you want me to wake you?"

Was this a trick question? How was he planning on waking her up? Did she want him standing over her while she was sleeping.? Needing to answer, she blurted the first thing that came to mind. "Would six-thirty be a bother?"

He glanced over his shoulder, one eyebrow lifted. "Will that give you enough time to get ready?

Anne-Marie nodded, nervous laughter bubbling from her unbidden. "It's not like I have any hair or makeup supplies with me. Heck, I don't even have a change of clothes. It seems as though I'll have to do the walk of shame tomorrow."

"Will you? I thought you weren't that kind of girl?" Richard turned fully to face her. He crossed his arms in a challenge, but the smirk on his lips spoke volumes.

Even though she knew he was teasing, she felt the heat rush to her cheeks. Not wanting to dig deeper into the hole she'd started, she cleared her throat. Holding up the teeshirt, she said, "Thanks for the pajamas. I'm going to bed now." When she reached the door, she added, "Alone!"

Rushing across the hall, she heard Richard's chuckles. Hearing him laugh made it worth the slight embarrassment. He had become way too serious during their discussion earlier. Hopefully, the lightened mood would give him sweet dreams.

She hurriedly changed into Richard's shirt, pulling it over her head and realizing it smelled just like him. When she crawled into the king-sized bed, she knew her dreams would all center around him. The wind beating against the window seemed to match the whirlwind of thoughts going through her head. It didn't bother her one bit.

RICHARD

Richard reached out toward his nightstand to set the alarm on his phone only to discover his cell wasn't there. Belatedly, he realized he must have left it downstairs. Leaving his room, he noticed the darkness under the doorway to Anne-Marie's room. She must have been more tired than she even let on. He was grateful to have her under his roof; at least he knew she was safe from jerks like George.

Once downstairs, he searched everywhere but could not locate his cell phone. Where had he last seen it? Fists on his hips, he shook his head in disgust. For the life of him, he couldn't recall. The last time he remembered using it was for that stupid dating app back in his office. Did he leave it there?

It's got to be in the car.

He grabbed his jacket from the hall closet and threw it over his shoulders. He could hear the rain pelting down outside and didn't relish the idea of getting soaked before going to bed. As soon as he opened the front door, he realized the storm was way more severe than a mere tropical depression.

It felt more like a hurricane. But that was ridiculous. Wouldn't he have heard something about a storm of that magnitude? Probably, if he hadn't been distracted by a pretty lady sitting in a wheelchair. Ever since she'd come into his life, he'd felt stuck in a whirlwind of confusion.

He ducked and ran for his car. The wind whipped the coat away from his body, allowing the driving rain to soak him within a split second.

So much for staying dry.

He even had trouble getting enough leverage to open the car door with the force of the wind pushing against it—definitely a severe storm.

Finally, giving up on the driver's side, he ran around to the passenger side. At least the car could provide some shelter from the storm's onslaught. The door opened easily, and he crawled inside and pulled the door closed behind him.

Like a storm cellar, the overbuilt Phantom felt like a safe haven. He turned on the dome light and instantly spotted his phone in the center console. When he picked it up, it buzzed in his hand with a hurricane warning.

"You've got to be kidding!" He clutched his fingers tighter around the phone. "Anne-Marie!" He couldn't leave her in the house with a hurricane bearing down on them. They had to get into the storm cellar and take cover.

He didn't remember leaving the car or even racing up the stairs. The next thing he knew, he barged through Anne-Marie's bedroom door and flicked the light switch. Only it didn't come on. The power was out. "Anne-Marie! Get up; there's a hurricane."

"What?" Anne-Marie's sleepy voice sounded in the darkness.

"Get up! Quickly! We don't have time to waste. Didn't you hear me say there's a hurricane, and we have to take shelter?" How come she wasn't moving faster? Didn't she realize the danger they faced?

"Don't be silly. It's just a rainstorm. Let me sleep, Rich."

By then, Richard's eyes had adjusted to the darkness. Anne-Marie actually rolled over until her back faced him. Not wanting to waste any more time arguing with her, he lunged across the room and flung off her covers. In the next instant, he pulled her from the bed and into his arms. This time she did struggle and squeal in protest, unlike that morning.

"What are you doing? Richard, put me down this instant!"

"Quit struggling, or I'll drop you." Richard's feet were already moving them closer to the stairs. He had to slow down as he descended, not wanting to trip and hurt both of them in the process. At the foyer, he turned left and raced down the hall until he came to another door. This one was made of steel and led deep underground.

Once he reached the bottom of the cellar, he lowered Anne-Marie onto the oversized leather couch. He grabbed a quilt and tossed it over her, knowing she'd be cold. He raced back up and made sure the bar covered the door.

He rechecked his phone, this time opening the weather app to see that the eye of the storm was almost directly over them. That was too close. He turned and went to sit with Anne-Marie.

"Will you tell me what you're up to? This isn't funny, Richard." She had curled up in the corner of the couch, her knees pulled tight to her body, and the quilt covering her all the way up to her chin. She looked anything but comfortable; her eyes glared at him from the illumination of his phone.

Rather than repeat himself, he scooted next to her and held out his phone so that she could see the storm for herself. "That's almost on top of us."

"That looks serious. What does all of the red mean?"

"Rain. Lots of rain." Now that Richard was no longer running, he started to feel the chill of the basement through his soaking clothes. A shiver raced through him, and he looked around for another blanket. Unfortunately, Anne-Marie's was the only one he'd packed in the cellar. He never thought he'd be sharing the space with anyone, so it seemed unnecessary to have more than one.

His teeth began to chatter uncontrollably.

"What is that sound?" Anne-Marie asked. "Is that the house falling apart?"

Richard had to laugh at her silly notion. "No, it's my teeth. I had to go outside to find my phone, and I got soaked."

"Here!" Anne-Marie pulled the blanket away from her and held it out toward him.

"No. You'll freeze without it. You're only wearing a shirt, remember?" He stood up and went to search for another set of clothes. Surely, he'd thought to pack extra provisions.

Anne-Marie tucked the blanket around her and turned to watch Richard as he stalked around the room. "What are you looking for?"

"Clothes. I can't believe I didn't think to pack anything extra. That's just plain stupid of me." He opened another box and found bottled water. Grabbing two, he held one out for Anne-Marie. His icy fingers touched hers as she took the bottle.

"Good grief, Richard; you're freezing. Get over here and sit. We can share this blanket."

Shaking his head, he said, "I'll get you soaking wet."

"Too late. You already carried me down here. Come on. I promise I won't bite." Anne-Marie held up the corner of the blanket and waited.

Not wanting her to get any colder, Richard made up his mind. Rather than soaking everything, he pulled off his shirt and dropped his pants to the floor. Thankful for the darkness, he scooted close to Anne-Marie's side and almost sighed with relief at the heat she'd already imparted into the thick quilt.

Anne-Marie's hand briefly touched his side, and she drew it back as if he had burned her. "What happened to your clothes?"

The answer seemed rather obvious. "I took them off."

"Are you naked?"

"Would you kick me out if I were?"

"No, but I'm going to keep my hands up by my chin. I suggest you do the same." The blanket tugged toward her as she put action to her words.

Richard laughed.

"What's so funny?"

"I'm not completely naked. I kept my boxer briefs on if that makes you feel any better."

CHAPTER 13

ANNE-MARIE

Hearing his teeth continue to chatter beside her pulled at her heartstrings. How could she do nothing after he probably just saved her life? There was nothing wrong with helping him; after all, she'd do it for a stranger.

Reaching over, she touched his arm. His skin felt rough with the chill bumps covering them. And she almost cried out in alarm; she'd never felt anyone as cold. "Richard, you're going to get hypothermia. Come closer to me. We can keep each other warm." She understood survival skills. After all, she'd been in the Girl Scouts.

Richard's sluggish response and his continued chattering made Anne-Marie fear he'd chip his teeth if it continued much longer. Since he didn't appear to be moving, Anne-Marie took charge. She lifted the quilt between them and shifted herself across the couch until the entire side of her body touched his. His muscles, rigid with cold, jumped uncontrollably with his shivering.

Several minutes later, she realized her new position wasn't enough. Without giving it a second thought, she twisted around until she could throw her bare legs across his lap and curl her body up against his chest. She flung her arm across his chest and hugged him tightly. Maybe she could blame the darkness for her emboldened actions.

Holding this position proved more difficult than Anne-Marie would have thought. A cramp in her side threatened, making her squirm. She lifted her torso to straighten out the muscles and realized Richard no longer shivered. In fact, his arm had come up around her side and held her close to him.

Without his shirt, she also noticed just how well-muscled his torso felt so close to her. Heat rose to her cheeks; luckily, the darkness hid it. Should she move? Richard had obviously recovered enough to hold his own. She cleared her throat. "Um. I should move. I'm probably crushing you."

Unexpectedly, his arm tightened around her, keeping her close without any effort. His chest rumbled under her ear where it pressed against him, and his heartbeat thumped with a slow, regular rhythm. "I don't mind. Besides, you hardly weigh anything. I should know; I've carried you twice today, in case you've forgotten."

Ugh, no. She hadn't forgotten, but she wanted to. Resisting the urge to squirm, she remained still. Rather than move back to her place in the corner, she pushed gently against his chest, already wishing she'd stayed put. It wasn't right for her to remain on top of him without any real reason. She opted to settle herself right next to him. Even as she did so, she missed his heat and the closeness they shared in his moment of need.

She should have remained where she was, but it was too late to do anything about it now. Richard seemed to sense her regret, or possibly he missed it himself because he kept his arm draped over her shoulders and pulled her close to his side.

Anne-Marie inhaled deeply, loving the intoxicating scent of him. Was it so wrong to feel this way about her boss? It wasn't like she had to tell him what she was thinking. He'd never have to know.

"What are you thinking?" Richard asked.

Anne-Marie burst out laughing. His timing couldn't have been better unless he actually could read her mind. Giggles persisted, making it impossible to answer.

"I wasn't trying to be funny." Richard leaned away, trying to get a look at her face.

Even though the basement was dark, their eyes had adjusted so they could see the shadows of one another. Where her hand still rested across it, his chest vibrated with his words. Anne-Marie could hardly catch her breath between bouts of laughter. Finally, she managed to spit out, "I'm sorry."

"For what? You haven't done anything wrong." His hand squeezed her bicep.

Several deep breaths allowed her to be calm enough to attempt an answer without incriminating herself. "The timing of your question was what tickled me. I was just thinking you wouldn't have to know how much I enjoyed spending this time with you."

"Really? You like being with me?"

"Why do you sound so surprised? Anybody would love this. Well, minus the hurricane. But, you know what I mean." Anne-Marie clamped her lips shut before she could say anything more ridiculous. She babbled when she got nervous.

Now that she didn't have to worry about Richard dying on her, the warmth they shared made her realize just how tired she was. A yawn forced its way out, and her jaw almost cracked with its intensity; she even heard the whooshing in her ears as it carried on.

Richard squeezed her again and said, "I'm the one who should be sorry. You're clearly exhausted, and I literally ripped you out of your bed and hauled you down here without any warning. Why don't you try to sleep while I keep track of the storm?"

She wanted to argue, but another yawn escaped. She nodded against his side and said, "Okay, but only if you promise to wake me if something goes wrong. Do you have your phone nearby?"

With a slight shift of his other arm, his hand turned over to show the lit display on his phone. "Right here."

"Let me see the weather app again now that I'm more awake." She reached out and pulled his hand closer. The brightness of the screen hurt her eyes, but the image it displayed worried her more. "That storm looks really big. Does this kind of weather happen often?"

"More often than I'd like, but you get used to it. We're lucky here; we're outside of the three hundred-year flood plain."

Anne-Marie shifted until she created some space between them to face him. "That may be, but the wind I heard earlier is going to cause damage, too. I feel like you should be more scared than you're letting on."

Richard's hand rubbed up and down her arm, maybe trying to distract her from her worry. It was working to a point, but Anne-Marie wasn't going to let this go. "How long will the winds and rain last?"

She felt him shrug. "Depends on the strength of the storm. Sometimes they blow themselves out, or they speed along and leave the area. With how quickly this one blew in, I'd wager that it'll leave in a couple more hours."

"I wonder how much help people will need come morning." Anne-Marie wilted back against Richard's side. His hand continued its rubbing motion, making her sigh with weariness and comfort.

"All the more reason for you to get some rest. We'll be of more help to people if we're not already exhausted. Close your eyes—the morning will be here before you know it."

RICHARD

Richard wished he could take his own advice, but his mind refused to cooperate. Rather than stew over his problems, he laboriously used one hand to operate his phone. Nothing could make him relinquish his hold on Anne-Marie, not now that she finally slept peacefully against his side.

He didn't know how this scenario had come to be, but he wanted to enjoy it for however long it lasted. Not that he planned on encouraging her in any way. He couldn't risk her life just because he selfishly wanted to be with her.

After several abortive attempts, he finally managed to open the app for the security cameras located throughout the Kingston Air facility. His heart sank with the first image. The aircraft which had been secured outside seemed to be a total loss. Mother Nature flicked her little finger and tossed his airplanes around like children's jacks. Luckily, he had a healthy insurance policy to cover the damages.

Switching to a different camera, he sighed, relieved to discover the warehouse containing his newest, most expensive aircraft had sustained little damage as of this moment. If his luck held out, then he'd only have to replace a few windows on the building. Each subsequent video showed less and less damage.

Closing his eyes, he whispered, "Thank you, Lord, for sparing me from total destruction. I'll do what I can to help those less fortunate." A wash of comfort enveloped him, and he leaned his head on the back of the couch. With a sigh of contentment, he allowed the stresses of the day to melt away and replace problems with pleasant dreams smelling of Anne-Marie's apple shampoo.

CHAPTER 14
RICHARD

Waking up with the warmth of a woman next to him felt foreign, but he wouldn't change a thing. If only the world outside could remain at bay forever, then he could be perfectly content. But that wasn't his reality. He had a business to run, and that didn't include getting involved with Anne-Marie.

No matter how perfect and beautiful she was for him. Or, perhaps, because she was everything he ever wanted, that was the reason he had to keep things professional between them. If only he could forget how perfectly she fit in his arms when he carried her, or how rosy her cheeks became when she got embarrassed. These thoughts weren't getting him anywhere but depressed.

He couldn't remember a time when he slept so well—probably before his mother left. Time felt irrelevant in the dark, windowless storm cellar, but the stiffness in his neck let him know quite some time had passed. Feeling the heat radiate from Anne-Marie made him reluctant to wake her, but they had to get moving.

He knew the storm had created a swath of destruction, but until they saw it with their own eyes, they wouldn't appreciate the severity. The damage to his commercial property would probably seem insignificant compared to the total loss others would face. Once again, he felt blessed to have created an empire where he could employ so many people.

His employees would need his help now, more than ever. If any of them lost their homes, then he'd make sure to step in and help them relocate. They were his extended family, and he needed to know they were safe and secure.

Nudging Anne-Marie, he felt her stir but not really come to any awareness. "Hey. It's time to get up."

"What? No. What are you talking about? It's still dark. Go back to sleep." She rolled away from him, grabbing the quilt and unexpectedly leaving Richard exposed to the chilly darkness.

Richard realized he should take advantage of her sleep to get himself dressed. Sliding away from the residual warmth of the couch left him covered in chill bumps, and his teeth chattered, reminding him of the night before. Trying to rush, he stubbed his toes on a box and cried out quietly as he jumped around on one foot.

Finally, getting his bearings, he located where he had left his clothes. As soon as his fingers touched the cold, damp fabric, he knew he wouldn't be able to put them on. He had to go back to his room and find something dry.

Looking back at Anne-Marie, he didn't want to leave her alone. What if she woke up and got scared? But then he realized if she woke up, she'd discover him standing there in his underwear like some creeper. That would be much worse, according to her previous statements.

Without giving it another thought, he sprinted toward the stairs. Hopefully, the house still stood above them, but there was no guarantee. Even with all of the hurricane straps and over-engineered building plans, Mother Nature could take whatever she wanted.

He pulled the bar from the steel door and swung it open. A sigh left his lips as he caught sight of his hallway, looking exactly as he'd left it the night before. Was it possible that he'd managed to escape the destruction?

Leaving the storm cellar, he made his way back to his room. Other than a couple of broken windows, some water damage, and a little bit of debris blown inside, he couldn't find anything else worth worrying about at the moment. When he reached his room, he tried the light switch, only to discover the power had not returned.

It was anyone's guess how long the electricity would be out. Countless houses across the region would be without power. Luckily, it wasn't winter, although summer held its own perils without air conditioning. Still, he'd have to go outside to find out why the backup generator hadn't kicked in. But first, he needed clothes.

This wasn't going to be a typical workday. An outrageously expensive suit wouldn't work at all. He needed clothes he could get dirty. Unfortunately, the ones he wanted to wear were already in the laundry, but what choice did he have?

He rummaged through the laundry basket and found the sweats he wanted. They didn't smell terrible, nothing a little cologne couldn't fix. Besides, he didn't expect anyone to be giving him a smell test. More than anything, he wanted a hot shower, but that would have to wait.

After getting dressed, he raced down the stairs and out the front door to check the generator. If he could get it running, then maybe Anne-Marie could have the shower he'd missed. Opening the front door, he stopped short at the destruction of his once-pristine yard.

As far as he could see, debris was piled everywhere. He even had someone's backyard trampoline leaning against the side of his Phantom. A shiver passed through him; he'd been outside the night before. Anything could have flown into him, but he'd been lucky.

The mess would have to wait—the generator came first. Trying not to get too distracted by the devastation surrounding him, he threaded his way over and around the mess until he got to the generator house. He had to clear the doorway before he could pry the panel open far enough to wedge himself inside.

Without any light, Richard quickly realized he'd need to take more time to get both doors open so he could see. Sighing with frustration, he backtracked and started throwing miscellaneous trash out of his way.

A child's doll stared at him from under a piece of plywood. The dress was torn, and the arms were filthy, but it struck Richard that some little girl might be crying for her lost doll. He picked it up and brushed it off, for what purpose, he didn't know, but he couldn't bring himself to leave it on the ground, forgotten, unloved, and alone.

With both doors now open, Richard could see almost the entire generator. Having been there for its installation,

Richard knew what to look for, plus he'd read the whole user's manual. The problem became instantly apparent. Someone had forgotten to turn on the propane. A terrible oversight, and one he felt foolish for not checking long before this.

Feeling disgusted with himself, he turned the lever until the tank hissed as the lines pressurized. Within seconds, the generator's computer activated, and the sound of the engine purring gave him confidence that his house would soon be back to normal until the power company figured out the overhead lines.

Richard grabbed the doll and closed up the building. He didn't know what he'd do with the toy, but she was coming with him. Maybe he could find the doll's owner—how far away could she be?

He opened the front door and stared. Anne-Marie stood in the hallway, her hair mussed, her cheeks rosy from sleep, and the blanket hanging haphazardly off her shoulder. She looked stunning.

"Hey, sleepyhead. I just got the generator started. You should have hot water if you want to take a shower." Richard knew he was babbling, but he had to say something other than how she took his breath away.

"How bad is it out there?" she asked, stepping closer to him. Her forehead creased with concern, and she leaned to look around Richard's body to see outside.

"It's pretty bad in my yard. I don't know how widespread it is, but we'll soon find out. As soon as you're ready, I think we should head out and check on everything."

"I wonder if my apartment complex survived. It wasn't that great to start with."

"We can swing by there first thing so you can get a change of clothes. But if you don't want to work today, I'd completely understand." Richard didn't want to think about not spending the day with her, but he had to give her the option.

I'd do the same for any of my employees.

"What's that?" she pointed to his hand, her eyes softening as she looked away from the doll back up to his face.

"I found it outside by the generator. I couldn't just leave it out there. It's silly, I know, but I thought I might be able to return it to its owner."

"It's not silly; it's thoughtful. Just the kind of thing I'd expect from you considering how everyone sings your praises."

"Everyone?" The side of Richard's mouth quirked up into a grin. "Does that include you?" He stepped inside and let the door swing shut behind him. The thud of the door made Anne-Marie flinch as if she came out of a daze.

Grabbing the blanket tighter to her chest, she took a step back. "I'm going to take that shower. I'll be back in five minutes." She twirled around, slightly stumbling as she caught her foot on the edge of the quilt. She caught herself before falling and grabbed the stair rail. With a nervous chuckle, she didn't look back as she raced up the stairs and out of Richard's sight.

ANNE-MARIE

She reached her bedroom, equally breathless and excited. The way Richard had stared at her both thrilled and scared her. Surely, she'd been mistaken. He was her boss; there was no way he'd be thinking of her on any kind of personal level.

Yet, the idea of it made her blush all over. She'd never be good enough for a man like him, but a girl could dream. At least she could say she spent the night with him, even though it had been purely platonic.

As the warm water poured over her body, she trembled with emotion. The past twenty-four hours had been a rollercoaster ride of emotions, from the strange encounter with George to spending the night through a hurricane, who would have blamed her if she felt like crying? Things like this didn't happen to her in her small Oregon town. What had she been thinking when she raced after Daniel to this crazy state?

But if she hadn't, then she never would have met Richard. The sight of him holding that filthy doll just about broke her heart. And he wanted to find its owner. Who did that? She did not doubt that he'd do it. With all of his money, he'd make sure it happened.

What was the real reason behind the doll, though? Ordinary men wouldn't think twice about a child's toy. It obviously stirred something inside of him, some tragic memory. Maybe, it reminded him of his own troubled childhood and losing his mother so young.

What gave him comfort back then? It certainly wasn't his father—he'd been quite clear about that much. Did one of his nannies become a surrogate mom to him? She fervently hoped so, for his sake, at least.

Anne-Marie didn't have time to think about Richard's childhood, not with him waiting for her downstairs. She rushed through the rest of her shower and toweled dry. Finding a brush in a drawer, she pulled it roughly through her long, straight hair and left it to dry on its own.

She found her dress and stockings on the bench at the end of the bed and put them on. Turning, she looked for her shoes. Finally, spotting them by the window, she reached for them and got her first look outside. Last night, Richard had told her the view would be spectacular, but she doubted this was what he had in mind.

Black water and floating debris filled the pool, trees were knocked over, and the gardens were destroyed. If things were this bad here, then what did the rest of the town look like?

Beatrice!

She needed to call her friend and find out if she were okay. But where was her phone?

She ransacked the room searching for her purse, but it wasn't anywhere. Straightening up from looking under the bed in a last-ditch effort, she had to conclude that her purse wasn't in the room. When was the last time she'd seen it?

In the car! She had to have left it there. She flung the door open and lunged into the hall. "Oh!" she cried out as she hit Richard's solid, muscular body with her own. The air rushed from her lungs as if she'd hit a brick wall.

His arms wrapped around her to keep her from stumbling and falling with the force of their contact. How he managed to stay upright was beyond her. "Where's the fire?"

"What?" Anne-Marie stupidly squirmed to look behind her.

Richard chuckled, the vibrations of it coursing through Anne-Marie's hands where they rested on his chest. Instantly, she recalled feeling his bare flesh the night before, and a blush rose to her cheeks. She pushed away from him, not able to look anywhere near his face. Feeling Richard's comforting arms release her almost made her wish she'd stayed put.

Needing to cover for her embarrassment, she sputtered the first thing she could think of, "I think I left my cell phone in your car. I need to call Beatrice to find out if she's okay."

"Oh. Well, you'll need my help with that." Richard stepped back to give her room to get past him.

"What are you talking about? I'm pretty sure I can open a car door," Anne-Marie shook her head at his strange remark.

CHAPTER 15
ANNE-MARIE

Opening the front door revealed just as much destruction there as in the backyard. She didn't know why it surprised her, but she'd never experienced the devastation of a hurricane firsthand. The news coverage didn't even come close to doing it justice.

Looking over to where Richard had parked the car, she realized what his remark meant. "Your car! Oh, Richard, I'm so sorry."

"It's just a car; it can be replaced. Let me get this trampoline moved, and then you can see if your purse is in there." Richard brushed past her and started grabbing trash that blocked his way from the trampoline. He made short work of it and finally managed to pull the mat away from the car.

Anne-Marie shook her head in wonder. Stepping forward, she said, "I think that trampoline protected your car. I don't think there's a scratch on it!" Wide-eyed, she turned to stare at Richard, whose expression matched hers.

"It sure looks that way. Who would have thought?" He pulled the passenger door open for her.

Spotting her purse and all of its contents spilled out on the floor, she sat on the plush leather seat and started scooping everything back into her bag. She could hardly complain about the mess with all the disorder surrounding them.

Grabbing her phone, she turned it over and sighed. "It's dead. Can we swing by her place on the way to my apartment? I'd feel terrible if she needed help."

"Sure. Let me get the keys for the Hummer. I think it'll get around better than the Phantom." Richard turned and jogged to the house.

"I'll get the keys for the Hummer, he says. Of course, he has a Hummer! He probably has a whole fleet of expensive cars at his disposal," Anne-Marie grumbled, not bothering to leave the car seat.

Looking down, she spotted the dinner receipt poking out of the top of her purse. Curiosity got the better of her, and she pulled it out. "Three hundred and seventy-eight dollars! Plus tax! You have got to be kidding me. It's not like we ate bars of gold. What in the world?"

Holding the paper out for the sun to shine on it better, she read the itemized list and discovered the majority of the cost had been George's wine. How in the world wine could get that expensive completely boggled her mind, but her anger flared all over again at the thought of him leaving her with the tab. He had to know it would be expensive, yet he'd done it anyway.

"You look like you want to murder someone. What are you looking at?" Richard asked, materializing from out of nowhere.

She held up the paper, her words colored with disgust. "Last night's dinner receipt. Can you believe George's wine cost almost two hundred dollars all by itself?"

"It doesn't surprise me." He plucked the receipt from her grasp and shoved it in his pocket. "As I said yesterday, don't worry about it. I got the keys. Are you ready to go?"

Anne-Marie's gaze followed the receipt until it disappeared, but then she spotted the doll. "Do you think we'll find her owner today?"

Richard shrugged, his eyes not looking at hers anymore. Without waiting for her, he headed toward the garage with six double-car doors. He opened the smaller man door and let it swing closed behind him.

Anne-Marie wondered at his sudden shift in mood. She hadn't meant to offend him, but he didn't seem to want to talk about it. Waiting outside, she hoped he'd open the garage door soon. Should she go after him, or did he need a moment to himself?

Seconds later, the door opened, and the red Hummer's engine roared to life. It didn't surprise Anne-Marie that Richard would have a flashy SUV; it suited him perfectly. He rolled to a stop right beside her and leaned over to open the door for her from the inside. He waited for her with a beaming grin.

Anne-Marie stood and shut the Phantom door. Well, if he could act as if nothing happened, then she could as well. Now, getting into the Hummer proved more difficult than she would have imagined. Again, she cursed the tight skirt, reinforcing her desire to burn it at the first opportunity.

Richard must have gotten quite the show of flesh as she had to hike up the hem before she could swing her leg up to the high foot rail. She must have looked ridiculous, but she managed all the same. "I really hate this outfit," she grumbled as she pulled the seatbelt across her chest.

"I love it." Richard chuckled and turned his attention to navigating around the worst of the debris in the driveway.

"I'm sure you do," Anne-Marie grumbled, hearing more chuckles from the driver's seat. She stared out the window, her mouth hanging open at block after block of mess, debris, and carnage. "Oh! Stop the truck!"

Richard slammed on the brakes, making Anne-Marie clutch at the seatbelt and the door handle as they swerved just before coming to a complete stop. "What is it? Is someone hurt?"

"No. I saw a puppy. We have to help it."

"A puppy? Come on, Anne-Marie. I'm sure it's fine. What about Beatrice? I thought we needed to check on her."

"That puppy wasn't fine. I think its mom is dead. Besides, Beatrice would understand and agree it's a necessary delay." Anne-Marie opened the door and unlatched her seatbelt at the same time. Forgetting how tall the truck was, she dropped to the ground and felt pangs of pain radiating from her ankle.

With everything that had happened, she'd managed to forget about the trouble her ankle had caused her. But now, it forcibly reminded her. Limping, she returned to the location she thought she'd spotted the small black and gray puppy.

Immediately, she knew the puppy's mom was dead. The blood surrounding her and the odd angle of her neck and back spoke about how she'd tried to shield her puppy from the flying debris. The puppy's head butted against its mom's stomach, but she didn't move.

Anne-Marie held out her hand, palm down, toward the puppy. "Hey, little guy. Let me help you." She slowly dropped to her knees, heedless of the dirt or the pain from her ankle. Her heart hurt worse for the puppy than any physical discomfort she might feel.

She heard Richard's footsteps behind her, and she called out quietly, "Walk slowly, Rich. I don't want this little guy to run." Wiggling her fingers, she encouraged the puppy to come closer to investigate. When he nuzzled her fingers, she swooped in and cradled him in her hand. "Do you have any brothers or sisters?"

"I'll look around," Richard said, wandering away from them. He carefully moved the debris away and found another puppy, but it was beyond their help, just like the mother. Another few minutes of searching came up with nothing, and Richard returned to Anne-Marie's side. "That's the only one we can help. We should go."

His choice of words caused her to look up at him sharply. Seeing the sadness in his eyes, she knew what he meant. Tears threatened, but she refused to let them come. This little puppy would get help; that was the best they could do.

They returned to the Hummer, and this time Richard lifted her into the seat. She gladly let him since she didn't want to stop cradling the puppy anyway. He passed her the seatbelt, and she fastened it one-handed. Wordlessly, they were on their way again, but Anne-Marie's heart broke for all of the animals who hadn't survived the storm.

"What street is Beatrice's house on?" Richard asked, his voice cracking strangely.

Anne-Marie didn't look up from the puppy. She wouldn't have known where they were anyway. Maybe, if she'd brought her car, she might have spent her evenings learning the town, but she hadn't. "She lives behind her business on South Post Oak Road."

Ten minutes later, Richard slowed the Hummer down, whistling under his breath. He rolled over some debris and came to a stop in front of Beatrice's Dog Walkers' business. "I sure hope the plywood is just there to protect the glass," Richard said as he turned off the engine.

"I hope so, too." She pulled her eyes away from the now-sleeping puppy and saw the mess outside Beatrice's shop. His trembling and pitiful cries were almost more than she could bear. "Beatrice will know what to do for this puppy. I sure can't have him in my apartment."

"I'll help you out," Richard offered before opening his door and dropping to the ground.

Anne-Marie couldn't even see him walk around the front. She shook her head at what guys considered to be cool. Downright ridiculous and impractical if you asked her. Her door opened, and Richard reached up for her. She unfastened her seatbelt but then worried about how to make this work.

He must have seen her indecision and said, "Just scoot out; I'll catch you."

She didn't have any reason to believe he wouldn't do just that; he'd already rescued her more times in two days than anyone ever had before in her life. Trusting fate and him, she did as she was told and landed squarely in Richard's arms. His breath rushed out at the impact, but his arms held her securely.

He turned, but before he could put her down, Beatrice appeared. "It's not exactly a threshold. What's going on here?"

"Beatrice! You're okay! I'm so glad. Rich, put me down." She squirmed, eager to get to her friend to ensure her well-being up close.

"Your wish is my command," Richard said, grinning over at Beatrice as he gently set Anne-Marie onto her feet.

She left him behind, her eyes intently scrutinizing Beatrice. "Is everything okay here? Did your window break?"

"You would have known that if you would've bothered to call me," Beatrice said, her hands resting on her hips and her head cocked to the side.

"I'm so sorry."

"Do you know how worried I was when I didn't hear from you last night? You said you were with a client and that you'd call me back afterward. I waited and waited. I even considered calling the police when you didn't answer your phone. I was worried sick!"

Anne-Marie knew better than to interrupt when Beatrice got into a rant. She would have to wait until she'd said her piece before trying to defend herself. Still cradling the puppy, she waited silently.

"And I see you're still wearing the same outfit that you wore yesterday. And you show up here with Mr. Kingston, and your hair is wet. Would you mind telling me what you've been up to that you couldn't call me to let me know you were still among the living?"

"It's not what you think—" Richard tried.

"I'll not hear one word from you, Mr. Kingston. I'd like to hear it straight from my friend if you don't mind."

"I'll tell you everything, but can we go inside? My ankle is killing me." Anne-Marie's weight shifted to her good ankle, and she lifted the heel of the one that hurt.

"And you come here with a puppy? What's this world coming to? What's wrong with your ankle? Oh, come inside already. I can see I won't get anything out of you until you sit down."

Anne-Marie followed her friend, and Richard followed her inside. Immediately, Anne-Marie knew why Beatrice was acting more overprotective than usual. "Where did all of these animals come from, Beatrice?"

Only a trail between crates was available to get to Beatrice's living quarters in the back. Anne-Marie sat on the three-cushion couch, joined by Richard, and waited for the answer.

Beatrice didn't sit but remained pacing the room. "This hurricane is wreaking havoc on all of the local shelters. I offered to help find out-of-state shelters that could take the overflow. You know, they can't adopt out the new intakes until the mandatory waiting period is up. Their owners might be out looking for them."

Anne-Marie nodded solemnly. This was getting to be a much bigger problem than she first realized. "How can I help?"

"Yes," Richard said, "How can we help?"

Anne-Marie glanced sharply over at Richard. She hadn't meant for him to get caught up in their problems. But the look on his face showed he really wanted to help in any way he could. A warmness spread through her at his thoughtfulness.

Beatrice swung around as if an idea struck her. "You have airplanes!"

Richard chuckled humorlessly. "That is my business. What are you thinking?"

"It would be so much less stressful for the animals if they can be flown close to the shelters where they'll end up." Beatrice seated herself across from Richard; her hands clasped tightly together as she leaned forward to see how he'd react to her statement.

"So you want me to fly all of those animals? Where are they slated to go?" Richard asked.

"Half of them are going to Red Bluff, California, and the rest are scheduled to go to Salem, Oregon. Would that be too much to ask? It'd really help out a lot."

Anne-Marie could see how much this meant to Beatrice, but she wanted to give Richard a moment to decide. "Beatrice, I thought you wanted to know about my evening."

Beatrice scowled at the interruption but then realized what Anne-Marie was doing. She turned her full attention to her friend, sat across from her, and said, "Yes. Start talking."

Anne-Marie used as few words as possible to tell about her disastrous date. She kept glancing sidelong at Richard to see if any part of her story angered him. Just as she suspected, his eyes flared with anger when she got to the part where George called her a hussy. He must have forgotten that she'd told him the same thing while they were in the bar.

Beatrice was properly enraged at George's despicable behavior and then turned to Richard, "I'm sorry if I spoke out of turn with you, Mr. Kingston. That was very rude of me."

"Please call me Rich. I thought we'd already cleared that up before. Anyway, I was just glad I was there to help. And I think I've got all of the details worked out for transporting those animals for you."

Beatrice jumped up, squealing with delight, loud enough to wake the puppy in Anne-Marie's hands. She hugged

Richard and then held him at arm's length. "I knew you were one of the good guys. Thank you so much!"

CHAPTER 16
RICHARD

On their way to Anne-Marie's apartment, Richard wondered what had come over him to offer his services. His guilt must really be taking over his good sense. After seeing the camera footage of the destruction to his airplanes, he would have more than enough to keep him busy at work without traipsing across the country, ferrying animals to shelters.

The sight of the dead mama dog and puppy triggered a long-forgotten memory—one he wished he could bury again. But the images came unbidden with so much clarity he could even feel the drenching rain all over again. Just after he turned sixteen and got his driver's license, he'd hit a dog. It looked nothing like the ones he'd seen today, but the blood pouring out looked identical.

He'd stopped to help, but the damage was done. He couldn't save the dog, but he could hold it until it took its last breath. The thought of leaving it to die alone was unbearable, but the life slipping away in front of his eyes gave him nightmares for years.

If only he'd been driving slower. If only he'd stayed home that night, then the dog wouldn't have died because of him. So many regrets, but the outcome didn't change. He'd taken a life, and now he could repay the debt.

"A penny for your thoughts," Anne-Marie said into the silence.

His mind cleared, and he hastily glanced over to Anne-Marie while he waited for the light to change. "Just thinking about the pet taxi service."

Anne-Marie's light, contagious laughter filled the cab of the SUV. "Is that what you're calling it? It almost sounds like you plan on doing this full-time. That would be amazing, you know." She brushed at a dirt smudge on the front of her blouse.

"Do you miss the puppy already?"

Biting her bottom lip, Anne-Marie nodded. "It's crazy, huh? I knew I couldn't keep it, and I'd only known it for less than an hour, but he was such a sweet little guy. So young, and already he's had a rough start. I guess I can relate."

Glad to deflect the conversation from his troubling thoughts, he reached over and squeezed her arm. "Well, he's going to get adopted quickly. You heard Beatrice. She sounded very confident. Plus, they're all going to no-kill shelters, so you won't have to worry about him."

The light changed, and he turned at the corner. Up ahead, he saw police tape cordoning off a building. Glancing at the addresses, he got a sick feeling in his gut. "Uh, Anne-Marie. Please tell me that's not where you live."

She looked up from her lap; her body stiffened instantly. "Oh, no! That is my apartment building. What do you think is going on?"

Richard found a parking spot across the street. He helped her out of the SUV and supported her weight as they crossed the road. Two policemen stood inside the caution tape, and Richard addressed one of them.

"What's going on?" He tipped his chin toward the building.

"The building is unstable. Only residents are allowed inside to gather their belongings. We've got a list and time slots. Do you live there?" The officer looked Richard up and down, clearly doubting.

Richard shook his head but then nodded down to Anne-Marie. "No, but she does. When can we get her stuff out?"

"Wait! Get my stuff out?" Anne-Marie's body went rigid under Richard's hand. "I don't have anywhere else to go."

"Don't worry about it. I'll take care of everything. Do you have anything valuable in there?" Richard didn't want her to risk her life for things he could easily replace.

"Everything I own is in there." She turned to the officer and asked, "What do you mean it's unsafe? It looks fine to me. I want to go home. Can I go in there now?"

Richard felt sure she would have stomped her foot for good measure, but with her ankle hurting, she had to resort to putting her hands on her hips. Seeing her so riled up was quite amusing, but he didn't dare let her see him smile. He certainly didn't want to be on the receiving end of her ire.

"We have a slot open in another two minutes. Can I get your name and see your ID?"

"Anne-Marie Pickler. I only have my Oregon ID since I just moved here, and I don't have a car."

"That's fine."

Huffing with disgust, Anne-Marie dug through the jumbled mess of her purse and finally produced her license.

The officer made his notes and handed it back. "You'll have ten minutes to gather your things. An officer will escort you in and out."

"Can Richard come with me? I can't carry everything by myself."

"Yes, ma'am. Wait just over there. We'll call your name when it's time." The officer pointed to the left and then redirected his attention to another angry resident.

"I can't believe this! Could my life get any worse? I guess I should think about heading back to Oregon. It doesn't seem like I'm supposed to stay here." Anne-Marie's eyes brimmed with tears. She crossed her arms and refused to look at Richard.

He hoped she didn't mean what she said about leaving. Even though he knew he couldn't be with her in the way she probably needed, he didn't want to see her go, either. "But that would leave me without an executive assistant. How can you even think about leaving me in the lurch like that?" He meant to tease her, but his tone came out a bit too firm for humor.

"Oh, Richard, I'm so sorry. I can be so selfish sometimes. We don't even know how badly your business was hit, and here I am complaining about my stupid apartment. I found this dump to live in, and I can find another place even easier now with the ridiculous salary you're paying me. Of course I'll stay."

"Anne-Marie Pickler!" The second officer called out.

She raised her hand, and Richard escorted her to the caution tape line. The officer lifted the yellow plastic, and they ducked under it.

"Ten minutes. The officer is waiting at the entrance."

"They sure are bossy," Anne-Marie whispered to Richard before they reached the entrance, but far enough away from the first two officers they had already encountered. She limped forward until they stood at the entrance.

"Apartment number?"

"231."

"Elevator's out. Only one trip is allowed today. Be sure you get any medications, pets, or valuables. We can't guarantee you'll be able to go back in after today." With her speech done, she turned and walked inside the building. She didn't even bother looking back to see if they followed.

By the fourth step, Richard had seen enough. Rather than argue with her, he simply grabbed her up into his arms. They made much faster progress once he took charge. "We can't use up all ten minutes just getting to your apartment," he whispered. The officer ahead of them merely grunted her disapproval but didn't say anything.

Anne-Marie's arms rested comfortably around his neck. He liked feeling needed and appreciated. It wasn't something he'd felt very often. Plus, Anne-Marie didn't gush over him about it afterward, which made the experience all the more enjoyable.

When they reached her apartment, Richard had to set Anne-Marie down. She fished out her key and unlocked the door. After turning the knob, she couldn't get it to open.

"Let me try," Richard offered. After watching her, he noticed the crack above the doorway. Applying his shoulder, he used his weight to force the door open far enough to let them enter.

The officer remained outside but said, "Ten minutes. Remember, others are waiting to get their stuff, too." She tapped her watch as if to prove some point.

Anne-Marie nodded and hobbled through her living room to get to the bedroom. "Luckily, I didn't have time to unpack the clothes I bought with Beatrice a couple of days ago. Those bags are already packed and ready to go. If you'll just put them by the door, then we won't be tripping over them."

Richard liked how Anne-Marie took charge of the job. She could have been wringing her hands and crying over the situation, but she had a plan. He grabbed the bags, moved them, and returned to see how he could help in the bedroom.

Seeing the shabbiness of the apartment made him glad she'd have to leave there. Thinking about her spending time alone in this neighborhood made his protective instincts fire into overdrive. Now, she'd have to move, and he'd make sure she found someplace much more suitable. Maybe he had a solution for her.

She dragged a suitcase out from under the bed and began dumping the small drawers straight into it. She didn't dither or complain about her clothes getting wrinkled, much like he'd heard Lillith bemoan too many times to count. She moved methodically, almost as if she had a lot of practice leaving in a hurry.

Once she had her hands overflowing with bathroom supplies, she dropped the load on the already full suitcase. Anne-Marie pulled the lid over and started to zip it closed. It refused to budge past the corner. She pulled it to the floor and sat on it before Richard could even offer his assistance.

With a triumphant cry, the zipper slid over the corner and joined with the other half in the middle. Awkwardly, she stood on one foot, leaned over, and pulled the suitcase up onto its wheels. "That's it!" she cried out, using the back of her hand to wipe away the errant strands of hair sticking to her chapstick.

"Are you sure? I mean, I think we still have a couple of minutes left for you to look around." Richard couldn't imagine packing up his entire life into one suitcase. But, he hadn't just moved across the country to chase a love interest. As she'd said before, she hadn't been here very long, so she hadn't had time to accumulate much.

"Don't need it. That's everything. Let's get out of this dump." She rolled the suitcase ahead of her.

Richard reached over and snagged it from her. "I'll get that. You're going to need both hands to hold the railing on the way down the stairs. It looks like I'm going to be a proper pack mule if we're going to get all your bags down in one trip." He grinned to make sure she knew he wasn't bothered at all about the task.

"I'm not going to miss a single thing about this place. It was all I could afford when Daniel proved to be such a...never mind. Anyway, let's go." She limped ahead of Richard out the bedroom door.

The officer popped her head in and said, "Time's up. Let's go."

"We're ready," Anne-Marie said. She bent to get a couple of bags before Richard cleared his throat behind her.

"I got it! You just get yourself safely down the stairs."

"Okay, okay. Jeesh! Pushy much?" She giggled and stepped into the hallway to wait for Richard to bring all her stuff out. Just as he pulled the final bags through the partially open door, Anne-Marie's body stiffened.

"Oh!" she exclaimed. "I forgot something!"

"No, we've got to go," the officer repeated. "I warned you to get everything. Let's move."

"I'm not leaving without my money. I forgot it in the couch cushion. You can watch me get it, but we'll spend more time arguing about it here in the hall than if I just went in and got it." Anne-Marie glared with her hands on her hips. "It's every dime I own. Please."

"Fine. Hurry up!" The officer actually sighed before glancing at her watch once again.

Seconds later, Anne-Marie returned, a white envelope clasped in her hand. "Thank you for being so understanding. I hid it for safekeeping. I can't believe I almost forgot it in there."

"Good thing you remembered when you did. We need to hurry, or else I'm going to get in trouble." The lady held her arms out as if she were herding chickens and practically pushed them along the hallway to the stairwell.

They made slower progress out of the building, but Richard managed to get her bags and suitcase arranged in the back of the Hummer, and then he lifted Anne-Marie back into the passenger seat. He'd consider keeping this vehicle forever if it meant he could keep using it as an excuse to have her wrap her arms around his neck.

Closing the door behind him, he gripped the steering wheel and said, "Now, it's time to see how much work we have at the office. Are you ready?"

"Yep. But maybe we can stop at the pharmacy to get me an ankle brace. I won't be too much help if I can't walk."

"There's always the wheelchair." Richard devilishly grinned, turning his gaze away from her fierce glare to start the SUV. "Pharmacy, it is, then!"

CHAPTER 17
ANNE-MARIE

Anne-Marie felt ridiculous wearing a fancy outfit, an ankle brace, and a pair of worn sneakers. But at least she could walk unassisted. Richard assured her she could change her clothes once they got to work, but first, she'd have to do the walk of shame. Not the most auspicious of beginnings at a new job.

"The building doesn't look like it's damaged," Anne-Marie pointed out when they parked.

"Yeah. That's lucky. If only we could say the same for the aircraft outside."

Anne-Marie glanced sharply at Richard. "What do you know? Did one of your employees call you about it already?"

Richard wouldn't make eye contact. "No. I saw it last night on the closed-circuit security system."

"Oh, Rich. How bad is it? Why didn't you say anything before now?" She felt terrible that she'd been asking him to drive her all over town while he had a crisis going on here. If only he'd said something, then maybe…she stopped that line of thinking. Nothing would have changed unless he sent her on her way alone. "I could have called Wilson so you could come here."

"I made my choice. I wanted to be with you."

Something clenched inside Anne-Marie's heart. What was he really saying? Did he have the same kinds of feelings for her that she had for him? If so, why didn't he just come out and tell her?

"Why do you think I wore these grubby sweats?" Richard plucked the front of his shirt. "I knew I'd be down in the trenches today, getting things sorted."

Anne-Marie held back an untimely giggle. This wasn't a laughing matter, but his idea of grubby was undoubtedly humorous. His outfit probably cost more than the most expensive suit she'd bought with Beatrice. Still, she finally put all the pieces together, now that he pointed them out to her.

She despised feeling stupid, and to have him spell it out for her certainly drove home how self-centered she'd been since coming to Texas. That was going to change today. From this point forward, she was going to think of others first. "How can I help you? This may only be my second day on the job, but I can take directions really well."

"Thanks. I think we need to find out how many of the employees made it to work today. Then I want you to call all of those who didn't come in and find out what help they need. Housing, clothes, food, transportation, everything. Write it all down and bring it in to me when you're done."

Anne-Marie felt like a bobblehead doll as she sat there, nodding away. She regretted not having a notepad with her. She'd have to memorize everything. "What should I change into?"

"Your dog-walking uniform is perfect, or something equivalent. Get changed, and meet me in my office in ten minutes. Okay?" Richard left the truck and strode into his fancy building.

His confidence in her bolstered her desire to make him proud. She had to prove her worth to him if it were the last thing she did. Ten minutes would fly by, especially since she'd have to dig through her suitcase in the back to find the right clothes.

Rather than attempt to get out, open the back, and climb up again to search her bags, she opted to crawl through the cab, over the rear seat, and into the cargo area. Not the most dignified maneuver, but it saved time. Besides, she doubted anyone could see inside the darkly tinted windows.

Should she dare change her clothes in the cargo area as well? The more she thought about it, the more the idea appealed to her. Nobody would have to know that she'd spent the night with Richard. She could keep their secret and her work reputation.

Wriggling out of her skirt proved more difficult than she would have imagined. Who knew how often you used an ankle until it hurt to put any pressure on it? Soon enough, she sat in the cargo area in only her bra and panties, a fine sheen of sweat covering her body.

The day was getting warm, and the SUV's interior was starting to draw that heat inside like an oven. She'd have to hurry or be dripping wet by the time she finished. Rummaging through her bag, she located a shirt that would work and swiftly put it on.

She kept digging to find her jeans. Her ten minutes were probably getting close to being up, and she cried out with frustration at where the jeans had ended up. Why weren't they with the other pants?

Her fingers felt the rough fabric of denim, and she pulled the offending garment out of the very bottom of the pile.

Shaking it in front of her like an errant child, she looked back at her suitcase and had to laugh. It looked like a bomb went off back there; her clothes were covering every surface.

She didn't have time to worry about the mess; she needed to get dressed. Lying back, she flung her legs in the air, the only space available, and pulled her pants up her legs. Just as she lifted her behind to finish the process, the cargo door opened, and Richard's shocked expression made Anne-Marie burst out laughing.

It was either laugh or cry. After all, Richard had already been witness to her most embarrassing moments. Why not add another one? She seemed to be a trouble magnet these days, and she had to roll with the punches.

"What happened back here?" Richard's gaze traveled over the disaster.

"I finally found my jeans," Anne-Marie quietly said. She finished fastening her jeans, sat up, and put her ankle brace back on. She slid her sneakers back on and scooted over to the edge of the door. "You're just in time to help me down."

"I'm getting pretty good at this." He grabbed her and gently placed her feet on the ground. "You're soaking wet. Do you want to find another change of clothes before we go inside?"

Looking over at her disaster, she shrugged. "Nah. It's not worth the struggle. I'm sorry I took so long that you had to come and find me. It seems like you're always coming to my rescue." She turned away, "Even when I'm in varying states of undress."

"What's that?" Richard asked, slamming the cargo door and turning to face her.

"Nothing. Tell me about the damage you've discovered so far." Anne-Marie took a tentative step with her brace and found it was quite comfortable now. Feeling more confident, she walked faster while Richard detailed the loss of seven aircraft on the tarmac.

"And you have insurance to cover them completely, right?" More mental notes were added to Anne-Marie's list.

"Yep. And it turns out that Jimmy already talked with all of the employees. He called everyone, so you won't need to do that. When David and John come up to the office, send them right in, okay?" Richard left her to go into his office.

Anne-Marie sat at her desk and looked through the files to find the insurance agent's information. The phone rang, and she started fielding call after call. As word got out about the hurricane, customers wanted to know if their orders would be delayed.

Not having any concrete information for any of them, she took their numbers and assured them she'd call them back as soon as she knew something. Most of them were nice about it, but some were downright rude. She put frowny faces on their notes only because it made her feel better to acknowledge their unpleasant behavior.

Two men entered the office between calls. She finally got to meet the two pilots on staff. "Go ahead. Rich is expecting you," she said, pointing to his office as her phone rang again.

Before she knew it, two hours had passed. Her stomach growled loudly, and she pressed her hand against it as if that would make any difference. She stood to check the refrigerator for a snack when Richard's office door opened. The three men exited the room together. Only Richard stayed and made a beeline for Anne-Marie's destination while the other two men left in the elevator.

"Did you get everything squared away with them?" Anne-Marie asked politely. She had no idea what their meeting was about, but she thought it was nice to ask.

"Yep. How would you feel about going on a flight?" Richard leaned against the counter with his hip; he crossed his arms high on his chest and grinned down at her.

"When?" Anne-Marie didn't know how to react. It was only her second day, but she loved flying. How could she possibly turn down such an opportunity?

"Right now." He grinned wider, enjoying the moment entirely too much.

"Seriously? Where am I going?"

"We are taking those animals to California and Oregon. Didn't I tell you I wanted to see Oregon? Now, you'll get the chance to give me the grand tour."

Anne-Marie stared at him, realizing he hadn't shaved in two days. The scruff on his cheeks looked entirely too sexy, and it distracted her. His eyes sparkled with mischief, which also made her mind whirl with desire. He looked just like the bad boy she always seemed to pick. "Well, move out of my way so I can grab a sandwich. When do we leave?"

"Wheels up in ten minutes. Feel free to bring the sandwich. We're not going to have time to wait for you."

"Wait. Don't we have to collect the animals first?"

"Already done. They're being loaded as we speak."

"Including my puppy?"

"Including your puppy."

Anne-Marie squealed and threw her arms around Richard. "This is so exciting! Thank you!" She went to plant a kiss on his cheek, but he turned at the same time, and her lips landed squarely on his. Pulling back so fast she almost tripped, she held her fingers to her lips, and her eyes widened with dismay. "I'm sorry, Rich. I didn't mean to do that."

"I did." He pushed away from the counter and sauntered past her. "Wheels up in eight minutes. Make sure you have your purse."

Anne-Marie stood in silence, watching him walk away. He had his relaxed confidence on display, but she was starting to see through his professional façade. What secret was he keeping?

RICHARD

Richard didn't bring up the kiss, nor did he acknowledge anything had happened between them. Instead, he led the way across the tarmac to the waiting jet. He gestured for her to climb the stairs ahead of him.

"Wow, this space is packed. Do you think they'll be okay like this?" Anne-Marie asked, still standing in the doorway and looking back down at him.

"They'll be more comfortable in here than in a cargo van or going as freight on a commercial airline. Go ahead and sit in the co-pilot's seat." Richard contained his grin at seeing her instant smile at the honor.

After closing the cabin door and securing it, he followed her into the cockpit and took the pilot's seat.

"What are you doing?" Anne-Marie asked. She glanced behind her in bewilderment. "Where's the pilot?"

"You're looking at him. Why are you staring at me like that?"

"I didn't know you could fly these things. I mean, I knew you liked aviation, but not like this."

"You're starting to wound my pride." Richard buckled up and started flipping switches on the panel.

"I'm sorry. Really. I didn't know."

"Clearly. Give me a few minutes to get all of the pre-flight checks done. We can talk about it later." He pulled his headset on and looked over at her with a grin on his face. "Or not. I'm just messing with you. Put on your headset, and I'll give you your first flight lesson."

"In this? Um, I don't even know where to start. Dad's airplane only had three gauges on the panel, not all of this." She gestured to the whole glass panel display with its flashing lights and graphics displaying every avionic instrument and redundancies needed for IFR flight.

CHAPTER 18

RICHARD

Flying always calmed Richard's spirit. The idea of leaving the ground and his troubles behind called to him all of the time. Lately, he hadn't had much free time to fly, and this was too good of a chance to pass up. He briefed Anne-Marie on the emergency procedures. "Now, pay attention while I make the radio calls and configure the plane for take-off. Once we're clear of this airspace, then I'll go over everything again in more detail."

The ground dropped out beneath them, and they climbed to an altitude of 42,000 feet. Richard set the autopilot and turned to face her. "Are you ready for that flight lesson now?"

Anne-Marie turned a serious expression to him. "As much as I'd like that, I'd rather talk about that kiss in the office."

Richard glanced back into the cabin to make sure all of the crates were still secure. He should have known this conversation was coming, but he wished he could escape it.

"Look, that was wrong of me. I can see I overstepped. It won't happen again."

"That's not what I was suggesting. I'm so confused by you. There are times when I think you might like me, but then you go and push me away when I try to talk about it. What's that all about?" She reached over and touched his leg. "I want to know what you want."

"Look, I'm sorry for sending you mixed signals. I can't ever have what I really want, so there's no point in discussing this. I promise to keep my hands and lips to myself from now on."

Richard wished he'd promised that to himself before he ever turned his head in the first place. That was a dumb move, but he still couldn't convince himself that he regretted it. If he had nothing else from her, he'd have the memory of that kiss. He'd add it to the many memories of carrying her around and her hugging him tight to her body.

He closed his eyes to try to stop the flood of special moments they had accumulated in such a short time. Nothing could sway him from his plans; he had to stay the course he'd set for himself so many years before. His father had shown him the problem of introducing a relationship.

"What's that supposed to mean? From where I stand, there doesn't seem to be anything you can't have."

Richard unnecessarily checked the instruments and searched the skies for any other aircraft. He had instrumentation that would tell him of anything nearby, but he needed to do something—if only to buy him some time. What should he tell her?

"Look, I can't risk getting into a relationship. It wouldn't be fair to the woman. Besides, I'm already married to my business. Who would want to come in second place to my career?" Richard cringed at how lame his excuses sounded. But some of it edged on the truth.

Anne-Marie sighed and shook her head. "I don't believe you. I've seen how you are with your employees. You take the time to get to know them. That doesn't sound like someone who wouldn't do the same for a girlfriend or even a wife. What's the real reason?"

Richard fiddled with the instrument panel and paused to listen to some radio chatter—none of which related to their flight. He wasn't ready. This conversation was happening way too soon, not that any time would ever be better.

"We've got a long flight ahead of us. I'm not going to let this go until you talk to me. You might as well spit it out right now. I might even be able to help. My mom always said I'm good at solving problems, so start talking." Anne-Marie slapped his leg to emphasize her point.

Rolling his eyes, he finally sighed. He'd tell her the problem, but she wouldn't be able to solve it. Nobody could. "Remember when we were in the storm cellar, and I told you my mom left when I was ten?"

"Yes." Her head tilted as if she were trying to guess where this was going.

"Well, that's what my father told us—that our mother left us. It was the reason he always said she was flighty, and also his favorite insult to assign to me."

"Let me guess; you found out something different? Did she leave your dad for someone else and start a new life?"

"Yes, I did find out the truth, but it would have been so much better had she found someone else. Maybe it would have saved her." Richard's hands clenched into fists. He wished he could have unbuckled and paced to expend some of the anger he felt rising at the terrible memories flooding through him.

"What happened? Was she sick?"

"Even that would have been better. No. She didn't simply leave; Mom was kidnapped and ransomed."

Anne-Marie's hands flew up to cover her mouth. Her eyes were so wide, Richard could see the whites surrounding her irises. "No," she breathed through her fingers.

"Oh, it gets worse. I didn't even know how bad until I was eighteen. I was looking through my father's desk to find the acceptance letter I'd received from Harvard. Everything was all set for me to get my accounting degree, and I was going to follow in my father's footsteps. I'd already been through orientation and declared my major. Father was so proud; he told everyone about it who would listen.

"But then I found a folder in Father's desk that had my mom's name on it. I'd never even heard my father mention my mother after she left, so, of course, I was curious. I sat in his oversized leather chair behind his desk and opened the envelope.

"That's when I learned the cold, hard truth. My father was a liar and not to be trusted. As I read through the pages and pages of police reports, I actually got so sick I threw up in his fancy trash can."

Even retelling the story, Richard had to swallow the bile rising in his throat. He'd never told anyone about this, not even his brother. In fact, he hadn't even confronted his father with what he'd discovered.

Richard stared at Anne-Marie's hand that now clasped his leg. The warmth of her touch contrasted drastically with the coldness he felt inside. He'd come this far; he needed to finish.

"What did the police report say?" Anne-Marie asked so quietly; it almost sounded as though she might not want to hear the answer.

Richard's eyes cut over to Anne-Marie's. Anger flared through him, making his gaze fierce. "Father refused to pay. The police report quoted him saying, 'I won't give in to extortion like that. It's the police's job to find her.' The police even noted that Father joked that the people would get so annoyed with her that they'd let her go."

He swallowed several times to keep from getting sick. As far as he was concerned, his father was responsible for his mother's death. Clearing his throat several times, Richard took a deep breath to keep going.

"Fishermen found what was left of her body six months later in a river." His words came out in a rush, but he still hardly managed to get the last couple of words out. Tears dropped from his lashes, and he pursed his lips to try to regain some of his composure.

"Oh, my gosh. That's the worst thing I've ever heard. I'm so sorry. And your father never told either of you that she was dead?"

Still trying to control his emotions, Richard shook his head. Hatred toward his father won out. "He was a coward and a liar. Do you know the police actually investigated him? They thought he might have hired hitmen to take her out and then stage it as a kidnapping."

"I'm sure he wouldn't do that." Anne-Marie's hand squeezed his leg.

"Well, I wouldn't put it past him. After all, he did get life insurance money once she was found. What I find inexcusable is that he lied to us. He let us think she might come back someday. I even dreamed about the day I turned eighteen, and I could start searching for her. I'd already booked an appointment with a private investigator.

"Anne-Marie, Father had enough money to pay that ransom and never even miss it. They only asked for ten thousand dollars. My mom's life wasn't even worth ten grand to my father. It's just disgusting."

"I hate to ask—," Anne-Marie removed her hand. She turned her head to look out the window; her bottom lip pulled between her teeth.

"What? I promise I won't mind. Nothing could be worse than what Father did."

Sighing, Anne-Marie asked, "How much money did your father get from the life insurance."

"A million dollars."

Her eyes widened, and her mouth opened into a perfect oval of surprise. She exhaled and shook her head. "Yeah, that doesn't look good at all. Why didn't you say anything to your father or brother?"

"At first, I was just in shock. I didn't want anything to do with my father after that. I moved out that day, in fact. I canceled my admission to Harvard and enrolled in a university as far away from Father as I could get. I changed my major, and the rest is history."

Richard slapped his hands down on the tops of his legs. It felt good to share that story with someone. Not even his college roommates or buddies knew what he'd been hiding. Nobody knew except Anne-Marie.

"So, you didn't say anything right then. But don't you think your brother should know?"

"I probably should have, but I waited too long. When Charles declared his major, he practically taunted me with it. You remember what I told you about his college days and now what goes on at his job. He rubs my nose in it all the time that he's Father's favorite.

"Even if I did try to tell him the truth now, he'd deny it. I don't know what Father did with those papers, and I didn't think to make a copy of them. Besides, Father should have been the one to tell us. We should have had a funeral for her, but Father denied us that closure."

Anger flared up in him again. He punched his fist into his palm, wishing it could be his father's face instead. Several of his knuckles cracked loudly in the nearly silent cockpit.

Anne-Marie flinched, but her questions weren't through. "What did happen to her?"

"I hired that private investigator to find her grave. I couldn't believe any of it was real until I could see the headstone for myself. But there wasn't even a headstone, only the laminated paper declaring the grave number and her name. Do you know, it's only a couple of miles from the house where I grew up.

"Father didn't even have the decency to get her a proper grave marker. But I fixed that, too. I had a beautifully carved, white granite marker made. Every year for her birthday, I take flowers to her."

Anne-Marie opened her mouth to ask another question, but Richard held up his hand to stop her. He pointed to the headset and listened as the air traffic controller directed him to change his jet's altitude and begin his descent. The distraction came at the perfect time. Richard needed to come to grips with sharing his mother's story, and he'd neatly avoided any more of Anne-Marie's interrogation.

CHAPTER 19
ANNE-MARIE

Anne-Marie's attention waivered for the rest of their flight into Red Bluff. She would never have dreamed that Rich's history would be so tragic. His attitude never gave any indication that he had such a toxic relationship with his father.

She couldn't even imagine living with that kind of story. Granted, her relationship with her mother was strained, but she couldn't dream of her mom killing her dad. Of course, her parents had had their arguments, but to the end of his life, they loved each other.

Hearing Rich's description of his childhood made her think that she'd grown up in a fairytale compared to him. She was Daddy's little girl. He didn't even try to hide it from her siblings.

More than once, she'd overheard her mom argue with her dad that he played favorites by taking Anne-Marie flying with him. It almost sounded as though her mom were jealous. But Anne-Marie held those days close in her heart; they were her favorite memories of her childhood.

Once they landed in Red Bluff, she didn't have much time to contemplate Richard's revelations. As soon as they opened the cabin door, the unmoving heat practically took their breath away. They had to work fast to keep the animals from overheating. Luckily, the people who had loaded them into the airplane were efficient. All thirteen of the offloads were organized together nearest to the door.

They didn't even waste time watching the cargo van leave the tarmac before Richard pulled the door shut. "Get in your seat. The sooner we start up the engines, the faster we can get it cooled off in here again. Hopefully, Oregon will be cooler than here."

Anne-Marie fastened her harness and saw the outside temperature read one-hundred and ten degrees. "I don't remember a time when it was this hot in Oregon. Like ever." She fanned her face, trying to get some air movement, but stopped when even that exertion caused her to sweat more.

The flight to Salem seemed like no time at all. They landed at the small regional airport and parked the jet in front of the FBO. Once again, the animal shelter had a van waiting to receive the animals. When Anne-Marie went to pick up the last crate from the rear of the cabin, she saw it was the puppy she had helped save.

Her heart clenched at the thought of leaving him here with strangers. He'd already had such a traumatic start to his young life. His nose poked out of the woven metal panel, and his eyes looked up at her with love and trust.

It only took her a second to decide about the little guy. She set the crate down and walked back to the cabin door. Fixing her features to neutrality, she called out, "That's all of them."

Richard looked up at her, a strange expression crossing his features, but he didn't contradict her. She remained standing on the stairway, hoping the little guy didn't cry out and give her away.

The driver gave them a friendly wave and got into the driver's seat. After they left the tarmac, Anne-Marie let out a long sigh. Immediately, she turned around and kneeled in front of the kennel. Opening the door, she pulled out the puppy and held him tight to her chest. Petting his soft fur between his ears, he kept trying to lick her face as if thanking her for a second rescue.

"I thought there was one more. Hey, is that the little one we found?" Richard joined her on the floor. He tweaked the puppy's ear playfully. "He sure is a cutie. What are you going to do with him?"

"I don't know. It was probably foolish of me to keep him, but I just couldn't give him up. Good grief, I don't even have a place to live. Maybe I could give him to my mom or my brother. Mom lives here in Salem. Do you think we could visit her and find out?"

Anne-Marie suddenly realized she only presumed they were staying in Salem for longer than the animal drop. "I mean if we have time. I'm sorry, I should have thought to ask what your plans were before I started making assumptions."

Richard's answering grin spoke volumes. "We can stay for a couple of hours or a couple of days. Jimmy is handling everything at work, so we're free to do whatever you need."

Without stopping to think about it, Anne-Marie threw her arm around Richard's neck. She only planned on hugging him in gratitude, but her body had a mind of its own. Not even realizing it, her lips found his. The scruff of his two days without shaving prickled her chin, but she loved it.

Richard's response startled her even more. He didn't try to push her away. Instead, he pulled her closer until she sat on his lap, and his arms were wrapped around her.

He deepened the kiss, and Anne-Marie moaned in delight. This was what she'd wanted to experience with him from the first moment she saw him. The forgotten puppy squirmed between them, causing them to break apart in alarm.

Anne-Marie giggled and lifted the puppy. "You have the worst timing, little guy!"

Richard laughed. "It's probably for the best. We need to see about getting a courtesy car from the FBO anyway." He effortlessly lifted her off of his lap before he stood. Offering her his hand, he waited until she got her feet situated under her before he hoisted her to stand next to him.

Once they were sitting in the car, Anne-Marie wondered if she should try calling her mom first. What if she weren't even home? Besides, her mom wouldn't want a puppy; she didn't even like dogs. What had she been thinking?

Her brother would be a safer bet, but he lived over an hour north. She seriously doubted Richard wanted to drive all over the state just to deliver a dog to a possible new owner. If only her phone hadn't died. Richard had kept her so busy; she'd forgotten to charge it.

Looking down at the puppy industriously chewing on her thumb, she didn't want him to go anywhere but home with her. Yet she didn't have a home. Should she simply stay in

Oregon? Her mom would give her a grand lecture, but she could always live with her again.

How pitiful was it to be twenty-six years old and moving back in with her mom? She glanced over to Richard to tell him what she was thinking, but he turned and grinned at her. No way could she do that to him. Especially not after his heartfelt confession with her on their flight.

"Where to?" Richard asked.

"This might be a bad idea. My mom never wanted us to have a dog growing up. She's more of a cat person." Anne-Marie twirled her finger in front of the puppy's nose, smiling at his attempt to catch it.

"That's okay. Why don't you keep him? You are clearly smitten."

"Yeah, that would be perfect. He could keep me warm while I'm living on the streets. Did you forget I just lost my home?"

"If you could call it that. I'd say it was more of a blessing to get you out of that slum. Besides, remember how I wanted you to call all the employees and find out what they need to recuperate from the hurricane?"

"Yes." Anne-Marie narrowed her eyes at him, suddenly suspicious of what he'd say next. If he even dared to try to buy a home for her, she'd get out of the car and walk to her mom's house.

"Well, you are one of my employees. You obviously have a need, and I'm going to provide a solution. So, you have a couple of options."

"Oh, this I've got to hear."

"The first option is that I pay first and last month's rent on a place closer to work." Richard's hands held the steering wheel in a death grip. "Or, the second option is that you come and live with me." He might have kept his expression neutral, but his body language gave him away.

Anne-Marie hadn't expected the second offer; she coughed and sputtered, but didn't reply.

Richard filled the silence. "You saw for yourself that it's a big house. You could stay in the room you used last night. You could even pay rent if that would make you feel better about it. Anyway, you don't have to decide right now. So, how do I get to your mom's place?" His hand hovered over the GPS unit in the car.

"We won't need that. I know how to get there." Anne-Marie jumped at the chance to think about something other than Richard's offer. Could she possibly live with him?

What would her mom say about it? Did she even want to introduce Richard to her mom? "Turn left at the road."

RICHARD

Richard hadn't planned on asking her to live with him. How the words slipped off his tongue was beyond him. It almost seemed as though someone else had taken over his mouth until the offer was out there. He couldn't take it back now, but he wished he could. Maybe she'd take him up on the apartment.

The idea of seeing Anne-Marie twenty-four hours a day made him want to run in fear and jump for joy at the same time. How could he be so conflicted about this? He had a plan, and it didn't include a wife. Girlfriend—maybe—but nothing more serious. He couldn't risk her that way. He cared too much.

He could still hear the sound she made when they kissed. The kiss that never should have happened. Already he'd broken his promise never to touch her again. Even now, he craved the feeling of her lips on his.

He liked how she came undone with his touch. She didn't have any ulterior motives, not like Lillith or any other girl he had dated over the years.

CHAPTER 20
ANNE-MARIE

Anne-Marie's trepidation over visiting with her mom turned out to be misplaced. Receiving no answer to knocking on the door, they used the stop as an excuse to let the puppy run and play. Emboldened, she took Richard's hand in hers and led him around the property, showing him all of her favorite childhood hangouts. At first, she felt silly, but Richard's animated expression and his peppering of questions spurred her to continue.

Belatedly, it dawned on her that Richard's childhood probably didn't look anything like hers. Where she had fun and laughter, he had only experienced pain and tears. Anne-Marie wished she could hold his ten-year-old self and tell him that he was loved and that his future was wonderful.

Wait! Was she admitting to herself that she loved him? How was that even possible? She hardly even knew him. But, if she were candid with herself, she loved the man he'd become.

Her mom always warned her of her hasty nature, but somehow Richard didn't seem impulsive. His thoughtfulness went beyond mere kindness; he genuinely cared about her well-being and safety—something she couldn't say about past boyfriends. Not that he was her boyfriend. Was he?

She stole a sidelong glance in his direction, and her heart constricted again. Her cheeks blossomed with red spots as she thought about their last kiss, filled with passion. Yet she couldn't help but think Richard was still holding something back, especially since he kept pushing her away. Was he afraid of commitment?

"I think we should return to Texas," she announced. Getting him back to his business was just the thing he needed. He didn't need a trip down her memory lane; he had a company to get put back together. She would help him sort it all out.

"Right now? Don't you want to spend some time here first?" Richard stopped, turning until he blocked Anne-Marie's path.

Remembering her earlier promise to stop being selfish, she shook her head. "We've got too much work to do." She gestured around the yard and added, "It was fun showing you where I grew up, but we're going to have our hands full with Kingston Air. Besides, we still have to track down the owner of that doll. Remember?"

"As you wish," Richard teased. He swooped down and grabbed the puppy just as he attempted to streak past them. "And we need to get this little guy situated back home."

"Have you ever seen the movie, *Princess Bride*?" Anne-Marie doubted it, but his answer surprised her. Was that a blush coloring his cheeks?

"Well, it might have been our nanny's favorite movie. I suppose I've seen it more times than I care to admit."

"Let me guess you pretended to be Inigo Montoya and wanted to avenge your mother."

"Something like that." Richard turned and walked away, his posture stiff, and his quick stride came just short of running.

The instant the words left Anne-Marie's mouth, she wanted to take them back. Watching the joy flee from his eyes almost broke her heart. How could she bring up his mom when they had been having such a good time? She should have known it would bring all of those hard feelings to the surface. The last thing she wanted to do was make him go back to that time in his life, the time when he felt unloved and abandoned.

By the time she reached him at the car, it was as if the episode had never happened. Richard held the door for her and handed her the puppy once she fastened her seat belt. "Have you thought of a name for him yet?" He lifted his eyebrows playfully before shutting the door and walking around the front of the car.

Anne-Marie's eyes tracked his every movement. No longer did he seem troubled or hurt. Should she bring it up again or just let it go for now? Her mind screamed at her to pick at the scab, rip it off, and let his feelings flow freely. But her heart told her to let it go for now. Besides, what if he changed his mind about taking her back to Texas?

Just the idea of never seeing Richard again made her stomach churn. Besides, she had an idea brewing, and she'd have to be near Richard to implement it. Once Richard turned the car back into the airport parking lot, Anne-Marie came to a decision. "I've decided to take you up on your offer of a place to stay."

Richard's hands clenched the steering wheel. Not quite the reaction she'd anticipated, but she pressed on. She kept the smile plastered on her face, even with the fluttering inside her making her wish she'd stayed quiet.

Richard cleared his throat, his gaze slowly moving toward hers. As soon as he made eye contact, he asked, "And what did you decide? There are plenty of amazing condos near the airfield."

She shook her head, "No, I'd like to stay at your house. I think it'd be easier for everyone involved if I could spend more time with you." Not waiting for Richard, she pushed the door open and let herself out. "Are you coming?"

Settling into Richard's house felt right—better than her original decision to come to Texas for a cowboy. A mantle of well-being settled on her shoulders. Her worldly belongings migrated from the Hummer's trunk into the bedroom across the hall from Richard's. Overlooking the debris-filled yard from her window filled her with sadness for all of the senseless loss.

When Richard called Anne-Marie downstairs for them to head to work, a surge of excitement filled her. Today her plan was going into action. It might have taken her a few more days than she would have liked, but her diligence had paid off.

Maybe now, Richard would find some peace, but only if her hunch paid off.

"You're in a good mood this morning. Did you sleep well?" Richard waited outside the Hummer door, waiting for her response.

"Absolutely. Remind me to thank your interior designer for picking out such a great bed." She fastened her seatbelt, turned, and her gaze fell on the doll in the back seat. Her heart almost melted when she noticed Richard had fastened the seatbelt around the dirty toy.

No other man would dream of doing something so sentimental; it merely proved how deeply he cared for everyone and everything around him. He reinforced this assessment with the amount of time, money, and effort he exerted into helping his employees recover from the hurricane's costly destruction over the past week.

Even their evenings spent together increased her love for him. Yes, she'd finally admitted to herself that she had fallen hard for the man. Hence, the plans she'd made for today would fix everything or blow everything up. She had to find the right framework to help smooth things over.

"What's got you grinning over there?"

Instantly, she froze. No way could she tell him the truth, but she wasn't about to lie to him either. "Just thinking about my day."

"Any hot dates I should know about?"

Unaccountably, his question felt like a dagger to her heart. Could he really think she'd be interested in someone other than him? Her eyes cut over to his, where she saw the mirth dancing in the twinkle of his eyes. "Ugh, don't remind me of my disastrous date with George. Nope. Unless you plan on taking me out, my plans are whatever yours are. Besides, I'm pretty sure your chef said we were having filet mignon tonight. I wouldn't dream of missing it."

"Ah, so Bobby's culinary masterpieces are the only thing keeping you around, huh?"

She paused, dramatically drawing out her answer. "Nah. I think the company is pretty fantastic, too."

His gaze didn't leave the road, but the muscle in his jaw tightened. In a low tone, he asked, "You think I'm fantastic company?"

Maybe he thought it was too quiet for her to hear, or perhaps he hadn't meant to say it out loud. She frowned, not because she thought he was fishing for a compliment, but because he honestly didn't know. "Of course. This past week has been amazing—the best in my life; if you really want to know."

They pulled into the Kingston Air parking lot. Instead of parking in his usual spot, Richard pulled the Hummer around to the side of the building. More than a little puzzled, Anne-Marie hoped he didn't plan on taking a flight. She'd purposely kept his schedule clear, but if he left, then all of her plans would be ruined.

"Why are we parking here?" The way he turned and stared at her made her want to squirm, but she held still with a monumental effort.

"What's going on between us?"

"Excuse me?" How could she answer that and not make a fool of herself if he didn't feel the same for her?

"When we're at home, I feel like you're attracted to me, but I'm your employer. I don't want you to feel like you have to do anything that goes against what you want. Am I making any sense?"

Letting out a long breath, she decided to lay all her cards on the table. "If you're trying to say that you like me, then yes. I think I'm falling in love with you. If that crossed a line, then I'm sorry." He kept staring at her. "Okay, I guess you don't feel the same. We won't speak about this again."

In a flash, Richard unbuckled his seatbelt and leaned across the center console. He pressed the button to unlatch her seatbelt before tugging on her arm. "Come closer. I want to get something straight with you."

She'd never seen this expression before. Even without conscious thought, she followed his demand. When the heat from his hands all but burned her arms, drawing her closer still, she realized his intention. She closed her eyes, more than ready for him to kiss her. But nothing happened.

Her eyes popped open to discover his brown eyes were ringed with green only inches from her own. "Aren't you going to kiss me?"

"If that's your desire, then I'd be honored."

She felt his tremors where his hands still held her lightly. "Kiss me, Rich!" His fingers tightened their hold.

CHAPTER 21
RICHARD

He must have lost his mind. He actually wanted to see where this thing would go with Anne-Marie. She said she loved him and his mind reeled with the notion. Sure, other girls had said they loved him, but he knew they meant his money. Anne-Marie never even seemed to notice his money.

Adrenaline shot through him as if this were his first kiss with her. Even though passion had flared between them on several other occasions, none of them had been coupled with love. This kiss would mean everything; it would change all of his self-inflicted limitations.

This kiss would bring Anne-Marie into his inner circle. Heck, he'd already shared with her the most intimate secrets of his life. That alone forced him to realize how differently he thought about her as a friend and confidante.

"I love you," he whispered, his lips brushing against hers. Tilting his head, he pulled her even closer, deepening the kiss and pouring all of his love into their connection. When she moaned against his lips, he almost lost control.

He wanted to breathe her in forever and never let her go. He should have thought this through better. The console began digging painfully into his side, forcing him to pull away. It was probably the single most challenging thing he'd ever done. "We should go back home. Nothing is pressing at work today. What do you say?"

The silly grin took over his expression, knowing he'd hit on the perfect plan. What good was being the boss if he couldn't take an unscheduled holiday? But Anne-Marie's posture stiffened, she wouldn't look at him, and he wondered if he'd gone too far.

"Maybe later. I really have tons of things to get done today. Can we talk about this after work?" Her bottom lip tucked itself between her teeth.

Richard reached over and placed his thumb on her chin, nudging her lip free. "Did I say something wrong?"

Her eyes flared wide, the brilliant blue even brighter in the morning sunshine. "No, never. I love you, too. But the timing is terrible." She lifted her hands and backed up until her shoulder blades hit the door. Her hand flew to her mouth, touching the spot he just had. "No, that came out wrong. Loving you is perfect timing, but going home right now is the problem."

Chuckling, Richard realized Anne-Marie was just as frazzled by their shift in relationship status. He probably should have stopped her sooner, but she was just so cute in her confusion. Taking pity on her, he said, "I knew what you meant. But, maybe you could tell me you love me one more time while I move the truck to my usual parking spot."

"We don't have to move. Why don't we just take a nice slow walk into the office?"

"I like how you think." He pulled the keys from the ignition at the same time as he opened his door. He hadn't even made it around the front of the truck before Anne-Marie let herself out and dropped to the ground. Disappointment flooded him, realizing he'd wanted an excuse to put his hands on her tiny waist as he helped her out.

"You should've waited for me."

She shrugged and held out her hand to him.

Instinctively, his hand went to hers; their fingers intertwined as if they'd done this a thousand times before. It felt right. His fingers gently clenched. "I like this." He lifted their joined hands and kissed her knuckles.

"I love you."

"I love you."

ANNE-MARIE

Could this day get any better? She wanted to call Beatrice first thing after Richard closed his office door. Knowing her friend, she'd probably have to hold the receiver as far from her ear as she could to avoid hearing loss with her squeals of delight. Anne-Marie chuckled and reached for the phone.

She'd only dialed the area code before the elevator dinged an imminent arrival. She noticed the time, belatedly comprehending it was later than she'd realized. Her surprise should be arriving right now.

But an older gentleman stepped into the grand foyer, his eyes never diverting to look around like most people did. Maybe he'd been here before. Anne-Marie set down the receiver and smiled pleasantly.

"Welcome to Kingston Air. Can I help you?" Her smile froze at the man's cold demeanor.

"Only if you can take me to see Richard Kingston."

"I'm sorry. Do you have an appointment?" She fumbled with her keyboard, full well knowing he didn't, but acting as if she'd checked.

"Is he here?"

"Yes, but you need an appointment, sir. Can I get your name? I can see if he has a moment."

The man scoffed. "The day I need an appointment to see my son is the day he's no longer my son." He strode forward, unerringly for the only other door in the room.

"Mr. Kingston, sir! You can't just go in there." Bolting from her chair, she held her hands up in front of him, blocking his path with her body.

"It's okay, Anne-Marie. Let him by," Richard spoke behind her.

Anne-Marie looked over her shoulder, relief warring with dismay. Why was Mr. Kingston here right now? She stepped aside, worrying her lip as she glanced at the clock.

"To what do I owe your inaugural visit to my business?" Richard's pleasant tone sounded forced.

"As if you didn't know. What did you hope to accomplish with that stunt?"

Richard's glance shifted to Anne-Marie. She shrugged in dismay. "Let's take this into my office. I'm sure you'd love to tell me what you think I've done wrong now." He stepped back and gestured for his father to precede him. As soon as his dad huffed past him, Richard rolled his eyes in Anne-Marie's direction before following him. He pushed the door behind him, but it didn't quite latch.

Anne-Marie wilted back into her chair. How could this happen now, of all times? What was Richard's dad so upset about? Surely, it wasn't because of her surprise. Only now, she hoped he'd be really late.

The elevator dinged again. Nope. No such luck. The doors swooshed open, and a younger version of Richard stepped into the lobby. He admiringly whistled as he nodded his approval of the décor. "Pretty swanky office," he drawled as he sauntered across the room. The stark contrast between Charles and Mr. Kingston's demeanor couldn't be more pronounced.

"Hey, did I see my dad's car outside? Is he here, too?" Charles leaned his hip against Anne-Marie's desk.

Anne-Marie opened her mouth to reply when Mr. Kingston's voice boomed from behind the nearly-closed door. She started to apologize but then stopped because she heard what was being discussed. Maybe this would help, after all.

"Hey, what's going on in there? It sounds like the beginning of World War III." Charles pushed himself away from the desk and started toward the office.

Once again, Anne-Marie sprang from her chair. "Charles, wait. You might want to hear what they're discussing."

RICHARD

"So what if I did hire a private investigator? It's not like you gave us anything to go on back when we were kids. I wanted to know what happened to my mom." Richard shook his head, wondering why this was coming up now.

"Look, your mother and I had problems of our own. I didn't blame her for leaving me. After all, I was practically married to my work. But, you've taken things too far this time, son."

"Don't call me *son*. It's not like you've ever cared. I've always been a disappointment to you, whereas Charles has been the bright and shining star you hoped I'd be for you one day. Well, guess what, Dad? I couldn't work for you once I discovered the police reports about Mom. All you had to do was pay the ten grand, and she would have come home to us.

But you didn't, and she died because of it. I wasn't about to work for you after finding out the truth."

"What are you talking about? You made your decision to betray our family when you were eighteen."

"Yeah, that's when I hired the private investigator. Isn't that what you were accusing me about?"

"No. I just got confronted by a media crew who had all of the details about your mom's disappearance. They said your secretary hired someone to dig up dirt on me. That's why I'm here right now. Don't you dare try to tell me that you don't know anything about it. Why else would that hussy out there do it?"

Richard felt as though someone had sucker-punched him. Rage warred with betrayal toward the one person he thought loved him. How could he have been so wrong about her? Her insistence on staying at work made perfect sense now. He'd let the idea of love blind him, and look where it got him.

He had seen his dad upset before, but this was different. "Dad, are you okay? Your color doesn't look too good. Why don't you sit and catch your breath? I don't know what's going on here, but I can assure you that I am just as surprised as you are to learn about this."

Maxwell's face almost appeared to go blank just before he slumped to the floor. Richard rushed forward, not soon enough to catch him. He dropped to his knees, desperately searching for signs of breathing. "Anne-Marie, call 911! Something's happened to my dad. Tell them that he's breathing but unconscious."

CHAPTER 22

ANNE-MARIE

Hearing Richard's dad accusing her of hiring the private investigator made her blood boil. Never in her wildest dreams had she contemplated something so underhanded. Besides, she already knew the truth, so what would be in it for her? When Charles looked at her with accusation in his eyes, all she could do was shake her head in denial.

She hoped Richard wouldn't think any of it was true. He should know her better than that after all the time they'd spent together.

"What's Rich saying about Dad paying ten grand to keep Mom alive? What police report? I'm gonna get some answers." Charles rudely pushed past Anne-Marie just as they both heard a thud followed immediately by Richard's call for help.

She didn't try to stop him; instead, Anne-Marie picked up the phone and dialed. Once she gave the details and knew help was on the way, she rushed for the elevator. If this were as dire as Richard made it sound, then they couldn't afford any delays—she'd meet the paramedics at the front door and escort them.

Memories of those last horrible days with her father flooded through her as she watched the paramedics load Mr. Kingston into the ambulance. Knowing how awful Richard must be feeling, she turned to him, ready to hug him and offer whatever comfort he needed. She lifted her arms, but he stepped back, his steely gaze directed at her.

He clenched his hands tightly at his sides, and his complexion darkened before he spit out hateful words. "I thought you were better than Lillith. I should have known better. Get your things packed. I don't ever want to see you again."

Anne-Marie stood there with her mouth hanging open. The words refused to form in her head, but her heart stuttered. How could he so easily cast her aside? He didn't trust her, let alone love her the way she thought.

She turned and ran for the elevator. This was the last straw and certainly beyond time for her to go back to Oregon. Even knowing her mom would lecture her for getting involved with a stranger, she wanted to have her mom hug her and tell her everything would be okay.

How stupid could she have been to think that this fairy tale ending was meant for her? Those things only happened in the movies, not for simple girls like herself. Tears blurred her vision, but she managed to grab her purse and call Wilson.

Wilson didn't ask her about her tears, but his sad expression from the rear-view mirror didn't help. She knew she should stay and defend herself, but it hurt too much. How could he compare her to Lillith? Hadn't he said she was just a shallow gold digger? Did he really think she was that insipid?

"Thanks for the ride, Wilson." Anne-Marie couldn't get out of the car fast enough. She'd had plenty of practice packing all of her things. It wouldn't take her more than a few minutes, even with the addition of the shopping spree items. At least she hadn't spent any of the rest of the sign-on money—she'd use it to purchase a flight home.

As soon as she opened the front door, Boomer ran to tangle himself around her feet. How could she have forgotten about him? Her mind kept stuttering with confusion. One thing at a time, she reminded herself. Scooping up the dog, she hugged him close and squirmed as the puppy tried to lick the tears from her cheeks.

"What am I going to do with you?" She set him down on her bed, hoping he'd stay there while she gathered her stuff. Of course, he hopped off immediately and investigated her every move. "Maybe Beatrice will take you in. She seemed to think you were pretty special."

Just the idea of talking with her first friend in Texas gave her some comfort. Besides, Beatrice would probably agree to drive her to the airport.

RICHARD

After getting over the shock of seeing his brother at his office, Richard wasn't surprised that Charlie got into the back of the ambulance. Richard turned away from Anne-Marie just in time to see the doors shut, and the vehicle start moving away.

He turned to go to his vehicle only to remember that he'd parked it out back. The reason for the deviation cut through his heart, but he didn't want to dwell on that right now. Patting his pocket, he found his truck key and jogged to the vehicle.

Driving faster than he ever had before, he caught up with the ambulance. At the hospital, Charlie took care of the intake paperwork while Richard paced in the waiting room. Richard's glance of his father being wheeled into the hospital gave him some comfort since his color had returned to normal.

He hardly noticed the people around him as his mind continued to replay the scene of him ending things with Anne-Marie. He'd been played for such a fool, and he hated himself for it. Never again.

"No!" The shrill voice of a little girl broke through Richard's tumultuous thoughts. He turned to see what happened to upset her.

"That's not my doll. I want the doll my mommy gave me. Only that doll will make her better."

The adult with the child looked frazzled like she'd come to the end of her rope. "Honey, we already told you that the hurricane took that doll."

Richard shook his head. No way, the chances of it being hers were astronomical. But he had to ask; he'd always wonder if he didn't. Striding over, he kneeled to look the little girl in the eyes. "Did your doll have a pink dress and purple shoes?"

The girl's eyes widened, and she solemnly nodded.

"Wait right here. I'll be back in two minutes." Even as he ran, doubt continued to plague him. This seemed too simple, unbelievably coincidental, and downright impossible.

Out of breath, he rushed back to the waiting room, doll clutched in his hand. He ignored the dirty looks from the people around him, needing only to get back to the little girl. He came to a skidding stop in front of her; the doll held out hopefully in front of him. "Is this her? I mean, she's a little dirty, but I found her at my house."

The girl didn't seem to notice the filth; her hands plucked the doll from him faster than he would have imagined. Rather than hug it to her, she fumbled with the doll's foot. "I love you, Izzy." The woman's tinny-sounding voice seemed to be what the girl needed. Then, the girl crushed the doll to her chest. Tears raced down her cheeks and landed in the doll's hair.

"Is your name Izzy?" Richard asked.

Izzy nodded.

Richard stood, feeling unaccountably happy about the reunion. He looked over at the woman who held the surrogate doll.

"Thank you," she said. "Izzy's mom is in intensive care. I'm Izzy's aunt. I still can't believe you had her doll, but God is good. He brought you here just when we needed you. If there's anything I can do for you, please let me know."

"No, thank you. As soon as I found the doll, I've been trying to track down the owner. I'm simply happy to have been here to help. Ah, I see my brother. Good luck with your sister." He smiled down at Izzy before heading across the waiting room to get an update on his father.

"Dad's asking for you. He told me about your argument. I can't believe what happened with Mom. And I can't believe you didn't tell me." Charlie began to lead the way to their dad's room.

"Would you have believed me?"

"No, probably not. The whole thing is stranger than fiction."

"Just one second, I have to talk with the nurse before we go see Dad." Making the small detour, Richard got the attention of the nurse. "Do you know the woman who is that little girl's mother and that woman's sister? She's a patient in intensive care."

"Yes. But unless you're family, then I can't disclose her name."

"I don't need to know her name." Fishing out a business card from his wallet, he set it on the table and pushed it toward the nurse with his index finger. "I want to pay the woman's hospital bill and have any experts flown in who might be able to help her to recover."

"Sir, I don't know..." she started. She picked up the card to read it. "Oh! Mr. Kingston, thank you!"

"Please leave my name out of this. Just send the invoice to that address. And, you have my air fleet at your disposal for bringing in any medical experts she might need. Just let Anne-Marie..." He couldn't finish the sentence, remembering his last conversation with her.

"Mr. Kingston? Are you okay?"

"I'm sorry. Just let Jimmy know that I authorized anything you might need. I have to see my dad now. Thank you."

"Thank you, Mr. Kingston." The woman clutched the card between both her hands, her eyes shining with admiration he didn't feel like he deserved.

Richard left the nurse, wishing he could have done more. He entered his father's private room, pleasantly surprised to see his father sitting up and smiling. Charlie had made himself comfortable sitting by their father's feet. "You seem to have made a rapid recovery. Did the doctors tell you what happened?"

"Nothing but a case of low blood sugar. They're getting my discharge paperwork as we speak. Now, about the matter we were discussing earlier…"

"I already fired Anne-Marie." Richard shook his head. "I can't believe she'd do something so underhanded."

Charlie stood, turning to look at Richard with a scowl. "Wait. You fired Anne-Marie? Why?"

"Dad told me that she hired the investigator. What choice did I have?"

Why would Charlie even care?

"I was with her when Dad dropped that bombshell. She was just as surprised to hear about it as you were. I know people. She had nothing to do with whatever this mess is all about. But, Dad, I'd like to know why I'm just now hearing about what really happened with Mom."

"Later, Charlie." Maxwell turned to Richard. "From the look on your face, you have to find Anne-Marie. Don't make the same mistakes I did with your mom. If you've found love, then you need to move heaven and earth to keep it."

Richard's gaze flew to his father's. How had he known about his relationship with Anne-Marie? After all, he'd only just admitted it to himself that morning.

"Why are you still standing here? Go!" Maxwell made shooing motions with his hands.

That was all the encouragement Richard needed. "Thanks, Dad." He raced from the room and pulled out his phone as he ran. After calling Wilson, he learned that Anne-Marie had asked to go home. If he hurried, then he'd be able to catch her before she even packed her bags.

He felt like such a fool for thinking Anne-Marie had had any part in that situation. He knew her better than that. Besides, she already knew his history. Now that he'd had a moment to think about it, it didn't make sense for her to hire someone to find out what he'd already told her. But why had the reporters said she was in on it?

Richard shut the Hummer door, and his eyes fell on a business card left in the cupholder.

George Hansen.

Of course! He'd threatened revenge. What better way to get back at him than to drive a wedge between himself and Anne-Marie?

Growling in frustration that he'd fallen for George's trick, Richard drove home, hoping he wasn't already too late. He couldn't recall anything about the trip, but he made it across town in record time. His calls to the home phone had gone unanswered, but that didn't surprise him.

He left the keys in the ignition and didn't bother shutting the Hummer door as he raced inside. "Anne-Marie!" he called from the foyer. Nothing but silence answered his call; not even Boomer came running.

"No!" Richard grabbed his hair with his fists and pulled until the pain helped him concentrate. Where would she have gone? She didn't have any place to go.

Beatrice! Of course!

After a quick search through the call history on his phone, he tapped Beatrice's store number and waited impatiently for the woman to pick up the call. A man answered, which threw Richard for a split second.

"Where's Beatrice?" Richard asked, too consumed with fear of losing Anne-Marie to be tactful.

"She's taking a friend to the airport. Can I help you with something?"

"No. You've already been a great help. Thank you!" Richard ended the call and raced to the Hummer. He should have guessed she'd want to go back to Oregon. Heck, he'd practically driven her to it.

Before he started driving, he made one last phone call. "Hi, Jackson, this is Richard Kingston. I have a huge favor to ask."

ANNE-MARIE

"I still think you're rushing things by leaving," Beatrice said for the third time. She held on to Anne-Marie and waited for her crying to subside.

"I can't stay here a minute longer. You should have seen the look in Richard's eyes. It was awful. There's nothing you can say that will convince me to stay. Not after that." Anne-Marie took the tissue her friend held out to her. She dabbed her eyes and then blew her nose. "Thank you for bringing me to the airport. Isn't it lucky that there's a flight leaving in the next hour? I can be home before dark."

Beatrice raised her eyebrows in answer. "I'll take good care of Boomer. When you come to your senses, you can come and pick him up."

"I really appreciate you taking him. My mom wouldn't ever allow a dog in the house, and he's too small to be left outside."

They walked over to the flight board to check which gate Anne-Marie would have to use. Even as they looked, the status for the Portland flight changed from 'on time' to 'delayed.' "Are you kidding me?" Anne-Marie cried.

Beatrice started laughing. "I'm starting to feel like fate is on my side."

"That's not even funny." Anne-Marie's hand clutched the handle of her suitcase. "I wonder how long it's going to be delayed?"

"We can ask at the desk." Beatrice's smile never left her face.

Anne-Marie rolled her eyes and followed her friend through the crowded airport. It had to be her imagination, but she could have sworn she heard her name being yelled. Frowning, she looked around. As if drawn by a magnet, her eyes locked on Richard's.

He swerved around people to make as straight a line to her as possible. What was he doing here? Hadn't he already said enough? Had she accidentally taken something of his, and he wanted to get it back before she left?

Then she remembered the black credit card. Of course, that had to be it. She began fishing in her purse to retrieve it. She couldn't look at him without a fresh wave of hurt washing over her.

Richard stopped just in front of her. She held out the card. "I'm sorry I forgot to leave this. Here."

Richard pushed her hand back, "Keep it. I don't care about the credit card. All I want is you.

"I was a fool. I'm sorry for the hurtful things I said. It was completely wrong of me, and I hope you can forgive me. I love you. Please don't leave. Stay. I'll spend the rest of my life making it up to you.

"I figured out that George orchestrated all of this. I learned about it too late, but hopefully, you can forgive me."

Righteous anger threatened to overwhelm Anne-Marie. Richard's words finally penetrated her numb mind. George had threatened revenge, and yet they still hadn't seen this coming. She wasn't about to let that vile man ruin the one good thing she'd found. "Do you still love me?" she asked, her voice barely above a whisper. She dared to let herself look into his eyes to seek the truth.

The look of happiness washed over his face. "Do I love you? My goodness, if your love were a grain of sand, mine would be a universe of beaches."

Anne-Marie frowned, her mind trying to place where she'd heard that before. Then it hit her, and she started laughing. He really was too corny for his own good.

"Does this mean that you'll be my princess bride?" Richard dropped to a knee and held her hand. "Will you marry me?"

Anne-Marie shook her head. "What are you doing? Are you proposing to me right now?"

"Only if you say yes. Will you do me the honor of being my wife?"

"Good grief, girl, don't make the man ask for a third time," Beatrice said, nudging Anne-Marie in the arm.

Anne-Marie could hardly form any coherent words. Instead, she nodded and dropped to her knees in front of Richard. She threw her arms around his neck and hugged him tightly. How had she ever imagined leaving this man?

He pulled her away, but only far enough for him to see her face again. "Thank you for making me the luckiest man alive." He put his hands on either side of her face and kissed her with more passion than she'd ever felt before.

EPILOGUE

(SIX MONTHS LATER) - ANNE-MARIE

"We should have invited George to the wedding," Anne-Marie teased. She kept herself turned away, unable to hide the mischievous grin, while she picked up the ball to throw for Boomer.

"Are you kidding?" Richard replied, his voice high with disbelief and disgust.

"Not at all. If it hadn't been for him, then you might never have come to your senses about marrying me." This time a chuckle escaped her lips. She turned her head until she could see Richard scowling on the couch.

"Maybe you're right."

"I'm always right. Besides, I'd say things have worked out better than we could have predicted." She tossed the ball and joined Richard, enjoying how perfectly she fit tucked up in his arms.

"I still can't believe you bought a private island and a yacht just for our wedding." She'd never traveled outside of the continental United States, let alone had an island named after her.

"Dad said Pickler Point and Zephyr were good tax write-offs. I couldn't pass them up."

She snorted and nudged him in the ribs, hoping he was just kidding. "Speaking of your dad—is he really okay with Charlie coming to work with you?"

Richard's hand squeezed her shoulder, pulling her even closer to his chest. "He said he was happy for both of us. I'm just glad we cleared the air about Mom. I think Dad felt guilty about keeping it all a secret for so long."

"I never would have guessed Charlie was so passionate about flying. How are his lessons coming?"

"Good. He's a natural at it. I'd say he's almost ready for his first solo. Besides, he might be eager to catch up with me—a little sibling rivalry."

"He's got the best instructor. Although I might be a bit biased."

"When are we going to continue your lessons? I haven't forgotten, you know."

"I'm not in any hurry. We've had a few other things taking precedence. What's another seven-month delay?"

Richard's expression turned puzzled. Before he could question her further, the gate bell rang. "That must be Markson."

"Ah, so he did decide to buy the Phantom from you." Anne-Marie stood and straightened her shirt over her still-flat belly. "I hardly got to say two words to him at our wedding. It'll be nice to visit with him finally."

⁂

"Dinner was delicious. My compliments to the chef," Markson commented, as they sat together in the dining room. Empty dishes surrounded them, and Markson picked up his coffee to take a sip. "You know, I got a call from a man named George Hansen looking to get funding for his airplane tug business."

Richard and Anne-Marie exchanged worried glances. "Please tell me you turned him down," Richard said.

"He really had a good pitch. But when he started talking smack about Kingston Air, I realized it would be a bad fit. Afterward, I started looking into his financials. That man's company is on the verge of bankruptcy. I think I dodged a bullet there."

"Definitely. That man's trouble with a capital T," Anne-Marie said, barely containing a shudder in remembrance.

Markson nodded. "If you're looking to partner with a tug company, I happen to know the owner of Best Tugs. Mike's a fantastic person. I could introduce you if you like."

"Thanks, man. I'd appreciate it. But only if he's already married." Richard smiled conspiratorily at Anne-Marie.

Anne-Marie's eyes danced, and she coughed to hide her chuckle.

"You two certainly look happy together," Markson said into the lull of conversation.

Richard glanced over at Anne-Marie, noticing how radiant she looked beside him. He couldn't remember any time in his life when he'd felt so lucky and blessed. "She's the best thing to ever happen to me. You should give it a try, Markson. Now that you've upped your game with the Phantom, you might have a better chance."

"Ha, ha! No, thank you. My bank account and I are pretty content with the way things are. Besides, I don't think a post-hurricane car will score me many points in the lady market."

"Well, it's not exactly the same as rescuing stranded puppies, but it can't hurt," he said, his hand going over to clasp Anne-Marie's where it rested on her belly. Only then did her random comment hit him. "What did you mean earlier about a seven-month delay in learning to fly? Are you pregnant?"

She nodded, her eyes brimming with tears and her bottom lip clasped tightly between her teeth.

"Congratulations, you two!" Markson announced, raising his coffee cup to them.

Richard leaped from his chair, pulling Anne-Marie up with him. He grabbed both of her arms, "Are you serious?" Seeing her nod again, he crushed her to his chest and kissed the side of her head. "You've made me the happiest man alive."

The End...For Now

Continue the series with Capitalizing on Love, Book 5, in the Billionaire's Bet Romances

Get My Free Book Now

To let others know how much you enjoyed this book, please leave a review at your favorite retailer.

To keep updated on upcoming books, visit www.amyproebstel.com.

Receive a FREE prequel story,

A Billionaire's Patent for Love

by signing up for Amy Proebstel's newsletter.

You can also follow Amy Proebstel on Facebook at www.facebook.com/ATwistOnReality.

About the Author

Amy is a *USA Today* bestselling author who writes sweet romance and young adult medical romance.

When she's not busy writing about endearing heroes, scheming villains, and Lone Star love stories, she spends her time binge-watching Hallmark movies, taking her husband and daughter flying (but not in the jets her billionaire's fly), playing with her Pomeranian and Pomskies, and cats, or reading.

A.B. Proebstel is the sweet romance pen name for Amy Proebstel, who also writes progression fantasy, epic dragon fantasy, and paranormal romance books that add a little magic to the world.

Please sign up for Amy's fantasy or romance newsletters on

her website at www.AmyProebstel.com or click Follow on her bio to get notices and updates when she releases new books!

- Get a bonus scene from A Cowboy's Recipe for Romance: https://geni.us/B1-ACRFR-Bonus

- Join her mailing list: https://geni.us/CleanRomance

- Join her Facebook group: facebook.com/ATwistOnReality

- Visit her website: amyproebstel.com

- Follow her on X: https://geni.us/Amy-T

- Follow her on Instagram: instagram.com/amyproebstel

She loves hearing from her readers.

ALSO BY
AMY PROEBSTEL

Billionaire's Bet, A Sweet Romance Series

Sweet Creek Ranch, A Sweet Romance Series

Wolf Shifters of Catskill County, A Clean Fated Mate Shifter

Series

The Chosen, A Fantasy & Magic Adventure Series

Dragon's Magic: An Epic Dragon Fantasy Series

The Rift in Our Reality, A Sweet Young Adult Medical

Romance